DATE DUE

JAN 2 6 2004	
MAR 1 7 2004	AUG 1 7 2010
APR 0 4 2004	SEP 0 7 2010
JUL 1 9 2004	JUN 1 8 2011
OCT 2 7 2004	JUL 0 8 2011
FEB 2 2 2005	NOV 0 5 2011
JUL 2 5 2005	JUL 3 1 2015
OCT 0 8 2005	OCT 2 0 2015
MAY 0 8 2006	
APR 1 1 2007	
MAR 1 3 2008	
OCT 2 9 2008	
APR 0 4 2009	

AUG 1 4 2003

The Message

Even the book morphs!
Flip the pages
and check it out!

Look for other **ANIMORPHS**®
titles by K.A. Applegate:

ANIMORPHS®

The Message

K.A. Applegate

AN
APPLE
PAPERBACK

SCHOLASTIC INC.
New York Toronto London Auckland Sydney

For Michael

Cover illustration by David B. Mattingly.

ISBN 0-590-62980-8

21 20 19 18 17 16 15 14   9/9 0 1/0

Printed in the U.S.A.   40

First Scholastic printing, October 1996

j

CHAPTER 1

My name is Cassie.

I can't tell you my last name. I wish I could. But I can't even tell you what town I live in or what state. We have to disguise our identities, we Animorphs. It's not about being shy. It's about staying alive.

If the Yeerks ever learn who we are, we'll be done for. If they don't kill us outright, they'll make us Controllers. They'll force a Yeerk slug into our brains, where it will take control of us, making us slaves — tools of the Yeerk invasion of Earth.

And I really don't like the idea of being under the control of an alien. I don't like the idea of being dead, either.

On the other hand, there are some things I do like about being an Animorph. Some very cool things.

Take the other night. It was late. I should have been in bed. Instead I was in the barn, getting ready to turn into a squirrel.

Technically, the barn is really the Wildlife Rehabilitation Clinic. My dad is a vet. So is my mom, but she works at The Gardens, this big zoo. The Wildlife Rehabilitation Clinic is just my dad and me. We take in injured birds and animals and try to save them, then release them back into their natural habitats.

That's where I was. In the barn. Surrounded by dozens of cages full of birds, from a mourning dove who'd run into a car windshield to a golden eagle who'd almost been electrocuted by a power line.

In another part of the barn we have bigger cages for the badgers and opossums and skunks and deer and even a pair of wolves who'd been poisoned. At the other end (far from the wolves) we keep our own horses.

There's an operating room and a couple of small recovery rooms, too.

Back to that night. Have you ever watched a squirrel in the park? They are constantly alert. Constantly looking around. It's like every minute of every day they're thinking, "Hey! What's that?"

So I knew that if I morphed into a squirrel, all that nervousness and fear would become a part of me. It's something we've all had to deal with: controlling the animal instincts, the animal mind that comes along with the animal body.

Anyway, that's where I was, in a gloomy barn with just the yellow overhead bulbs to light the room. Why was I there? Because someone, or something, had been sneaking in and getting at the birds. We'd lost a patient just the night before. A duck.

And because I couldn't sleep, anyway. I kept having these dreams. Only they weren't like normal dreams, somehow. More like . . . I don't know. Just really strange, that's all.

"Relax, Magilla," I whispered to the squirrel in my hands. "This won't hurt at all." I pulled some chestnuts from my pocket and handed him one. Another nut fell to the floor.

Some morphs are easy. Some are terrifying. When I was a horse, that was cool. When I had to become a trout, well, that was a little more weird. The whole time I just kept thinking how someone could fry me and serve me with tartar sauce.

And I don't like tartar sauce.

"Squirrel," I told myself. I always try to get into the feeling of what it might be like to be the animal before I even start morphing.

The first physical change was in my size. I

started shrinking. It's a very bizarre feeling. See, you feel like you're standing totally still, but the ground keeps coming up toward you. And the ceiling is moving away. Door handles aren't where they should be anymore. All of a sudden they're over your head.

I had shrunk to maybe two, two-and-a-half feet tall when my arms came sucking back into my body. Right about that point, the real Magilla tore out of there. He ran back to his cage, got in, and — I swear this is true — closed the door. Anyway, I still had normal (although short) legs, but my arms were stunted. I still had the normal number of fingers, but they were teeny tiny now, way too small for my body.

My ears traveled up the side of my head to rest on top. Soft gray fur spread across my body in a wave. My face puffed out and grew pointed.

Then, the wildest thing! My tail sprouted out of my body! And what was cool was that I wasn't a squirrel yet. I was still about half human, the size of a small child, and my tail just shot out, about two feet long! Much longer and bigger than it would be once I was totally squirrelified.

I tilted my head back and I could see this bushy gray tail arched up over me. Way cool.

My legs sucked in and I was down on the ground, down on the cement floor of the barn.

I suddenly discovered I hadn't swept and

mopped as well as I thought I had. Amazing what you can see when your face is just an inch from the floor.

Then the squirrel brain kicked in.

WHOA! YOW!

Man, did I have *energy*!

It was like I was plugged into a million volts. I was supercharged! My slow, sluggish human brain was just blown away by the sudden explosion of energy.

A noise!

What's that? I cocked my ears. I swung my head, focusing my big eyes. *A bird in a cage!*

A new sound! What was it? I spun around.

No, wait! What was that? And that? And the other sound?

PREDATORS! They were everywhere! I was surrounded! PREDATORS!

Birds! Big birds with nasty claws. All around me.

Wait. There was a nut. Oooh. A nut.

PREDATORS! Alert!

I scampered across the floor. Look left. Look right. Sniff sniff sniff the air.

Oh, yes. Predators. I smelled them. I heard them. Birds. A wolf. A badger.

PREDATORS! RUN RUN RUN!

Oh, wait. Was that a nut? I hopped over to the nut. YES! A chestnut! I seized it in my little front claws and began immediately to chew a hole in it. *Excellent! Wonderful! Chestnut!* And I had it! No one could take it away. Hah hah!

A noise! What?

PREDATORS!

Don't drop the nut! Run with the nut! RUN!

With the nut stuffed into my jaw, I ran.

I ran straight up the wall. Straight *up*.

And that was the moment when Tobias decided to show up.

CHAPTER 2

Tobias flew in through the hayloft overhead.

Unfortunately, in my squirrel mentality, with my human brain just barely holding on, I didn't realize it was Tobias.

What it looked like to me was a red-tailed hawk. A bird of prey. And this one was not in a cage.

No, this one was flapping around the high rafters of the barn. The hawk had talons like steel and a hooked beak that could open me up like a can of beans.

I felt his hawk's eyes on me.

RUN RUN RUNRUNRUN!

I didn't know what to do. I mean, me, the human being named Cassie. I didn't know what to

7

do. I knew I had to get control over the squirrel. But it was so hyper!

However, the squirrel knew just what to do.

ZOOOM!

I ran straight up the wall. My little claws grabbed at tiny splinters and cracks in the wood, and shot up at a terrifying speed. If you've never been a squirrel — and let's face it, you haven't — you probably don't have any idea what it's like to run *up*. The wooden wall was like a floor under me. But at the same time I knew the difference between up and down. I knew if I fell it would be down. It's as if you were running across the floor in your house, but if you tripped you'd fall back against the wall.

Very strange.

Tobias had come to rest on a rafter. But I could feel his eyes on me. I froze. I froze completely. Not even my tail twitched. I just clutched onto the wall and froze.

But I couldn't keep it up. That torrent of squirrel energy would not let me stand still for long.

Suddenly, with barely a glance to the side, I launched myself through space. I flew. I mean, I just jumped and hurtled through the air for what seemed like half a mile, but was actually just ten feet.

SLAM! I landed on the wooden beam that runs above the horse stalls.

Bad move. Tobias had seen my movement. Out of the corner of my eye I saw his vast wings open. He swooped down, talons raked forward.

But then . . . a new movement. Something large and furtive. A board in the side of the barn pushed open. A head poked inside. It was just below me. An intelligent, alert face, looking up at me and wondering if I was dinner.

A fox! Aha! My mystery bird-killer.

I had to get control of the squirrel brain. It always takes a minute in any new morph, at least, to control those wild animal instincts, but I didn't have a minute.

Tobias swooped.

Suddenly it was insanity everywhere. Birds in every cage began to squawk and shriek! The wolves in the next room decided to start howling. The horses were whinnying shrilly.

Tobias sheered away, startled.

Too late. I had jumped again, and now I was falling toward the straw-covered floor of a stall. Falling toward the fox.

I hit the ground and blew out of there, leaving a storm of dust and straw in my wake.

The fox came after me. He was fast. Very fast.

<Tobias! Help!> I yelled in thought-speak.

<What the . . . Is that you, Cassie?>

I dodged left. The fox dodged after me.

He was faster than me and almost as agile. Unless I could find a place to climb up and away, I was done for!

<Yes, it's me!>

<Well, why didn't you tell me?!> he said, sounding grumpy in my head. <I was considering eating you.>

<I just morphed. I just got control of this crazy squirrel brain. Now would you PLEASE save me?>

The fox's jaw snapped at my tail. I felt his teeth comb the fur.

<Good grief,> Tobias said. He opened his wings and came hurtling down, straight at the fox.

The fox saw the shadow of the big hawk. He stopped dead in his tracks.

Too late. Tobias raked him with his talons and shot past.

The fox decided this was more trouble than he needed. He bolted for his secret passageway.

Tobias came to rest on a crossbeam and looked down at me with his fierce hawk's gaze. <Cassie? Why are you out here at midnight turning into a squirrel?>

I was already starting to morph back to human shape. <Well, we've had some birds taken

in the last couple of days. We figured it was a badger or a raccoon or a fox, but we couldn't figure out how he was getting in. So I decided to morph and wait to see when he showed up.>

<Well, I certainly can't criticize anyone who wants to rescue birds,> he said. He fluffed his wings and began preening some ruffled feathers.

I was halfway back to human shape, growing up from the floor, feeling my legs sprout beneath me. But my human mouth was not back yet. <So, what are you doing here, Tobias? Looking for a squirrel sandwich?>

Tobias had almost completely accepted the fact that he was permanently stuck in the body of a red-tailed hawk. Recently he had begun to hunt and eat like a hawk. He was still a little sensitive about it, but I thought if I just made a joke out of it, he would realize I wasn't grossed out or anything.

<Squirrel sandwich?> he said. <No, I was thinking barbecue. Sorry I scared you.>

"It's okay, my friend," I said in my own voice. My mouth had formed. I was almost back to normal, all but this huge tail, which was still poking out of the back of my morphing outfit.

Normal, for me, is about average height, I guess. Whatever "average" is. I'm kind of solidly built, not skinny and not fat, with hair I keep short because I don't like messing with it. As my friends would tell you, I'm not exactly Ms. Fashion. Mostly, if you want to know what I look like, picture a girl in overalls and leather work gloves, biting her lip as she concentrates on trying to force a pill down the throat of a badger.

Jake once took a picture of me doing exactly that. He has it next to his computer in his room. Don't ask me why. I would be glad to give him a picture of me in a dress or something. Rachel could loan me the dress. But Jake says he likes the picture he has.

<I hear something,> Tobias said, suddenly alert.

I strained my ears. Human ears are so lame. Almost any animal can hear better. But then I heard it, too. A voice.

"Is someone in there?"

"My father!"

<You still have a tail!>

Too late. The barn door swung open. My father stood there, blinking sleepily and holding a flashlight. "Cass? What are you doing out here?"

I stuck my hands behind my back and tried to hold my big squirrel tail down while I attempted to morph it away at maximum speed. "N-n-nothing, Dad. I-I-I just couldn't sleep."

He nodded. "Okay. Well, go to bed now," he said crankily. My father is one of those people who needs about an hour and three cups of coffee to wake up.

"Okay, Daddy," I said.

He hesitated. "Cassie? Turn around."

"Turn around?" I repeated in a squeaky voice.

"Yeah. Turn around. It's . . . just turn around."

Slowly I turned. As I did, the last of the tail shwooped back into my spine.

"Huh," my dad said. "I gotta get back to sleep. I swear I thought you had a tail."

"Heh heh," I laughed weakly.

When he left I collapsed back on the straw. "I really should have just stayed in bed," I said to Tobias. "Dreams or no dreams."

<Dreams?> he snapped. <What kind of dreams?>

I shrugged. "I don't know. These kind of weird dreams about the sea."

<The sea,> he echoed. <And a voice, calling out to you from beneath the water.>

It was warm in the barn, but suddenly I felt really cold.

CHAPTER 3

"No, I haven't had any weird dreams about the sea," Marco said. "I've had weird dreams about my sheets trying to strangle me. I've had weird dreams about falling from way up high and when I finally land I'm in Mister Rogers' Neighborhood talking to King Friday. I've had weird dreams about that woman on *Baywatch* . . . hmm, well, that does kind of involve the ocean, I guess."

"You have dreams about King Friday?" Rachel asked him. She put on a worried look. "I see." She shook her head slowly and made a *tsk, tsk* sound.

"What? What's the matter with dreaming about King Friday?" Marco demanded.

Rachel shrugged. "All I'm going to say is you should think about seeing a counselor before your condition worsens." Rachel turned so Marco couldn't see her and gave me a wink.

"Very funny," Marco sneered. But he still looked a little worried.

We were in Rachel's room the next day, after school. Her room is so neat. Straight out of a magazine, you know? Like everything matches or goes together. She has this bulletin board where she puts little wise sayings on Post-it notes.

I drifted over to the bulletin board and read "'Don't think there are no crocodiles just because the water is calm.' — Malayan Proverb."

Just beside that was "'If you know the enemy and know yourself, you need not fear the results of a hundred battles.' — Sun Tzu."

It made me a little sad. In the good old days, Rachel would have had a bunch of quotes about being a good person or whatever. It just showed how much our lives had changed.

In a very short time we had all grown accustomed to a world of fear and danger. We had arrived at Rachel's house separately. We had each checked to make sure we weren't being followed. We had planned the afternoon in advance to be sure that Rachel's mom and her two sisters would be out.

We had even had Tobias fly over the area looking for anything unusual.

That's what our lives had become. That and quotations full of paranoia and battle.

Jake hadn't said anything yet. Tobias and I had both told everyone about our strangely identical dreams. About the voice that seemed to come from beneath the sea. The strange voice that called to us.

No one else had heard the voice in their dreams. Marco had made jokes. Rachel had been supportive but skeptical. Only Jake had remained silent.

I suppose you could say Jake is sort of our "leader," although he's not bossy in any way. It's more like this natural aspect of his personality. He's the one you just automatically look to when there's trouble.

Of course, I look to him for other reasons. Not that I would ever tell him or anything, but I really like Jake. You know, as in *like*.

He's very cute, in a big, strong kind of way. He has brown hair and dark, dark eyes. He seems very serious until you get to know him. And then you realize he's still pretty serious, but he also knows when to laugh.

Jake has to know when to laugh because Marco has been his best friend since they were both in diapers. They've competed and fought and disagreed the whole time. Marco's mission in life is to find the humor in everything. Even in his best friend.

Marco is kind of cute, too, although he's not my type. He wears his brown hair long and has these amazing eyelashes that I would love to have myself.

Marco isn't interested in being in charge, or even in being part of a team. He wants us to just quit the whole thing. He wants us to forget the Yeerks and forget morphing and just try and stay alive.

But at the same time, it's Marco who is very aware of all the security problems. He's the one who makes sure we never discuss anything on the phone, where enemy ears might be listening in.

Rachel is my closest friend. She has been for years. How can I explain Rachel? First of all, she and Jake are cousins, and they have a lot in common. They seem to grow strong people in that family, because Rachel is the strongest person I know. It's like nothing ever intimidates her. She's totally fearless, or at least that's how she seems.

To look at her you'd think, *Oh, she'll grow up to be some airheaded model*, because she's very tall and pretty and blond. But I pity anyone who mistakes Rachel for a wimpy airhead.

Sometimes I think Rachel likes the way everything has worked out. It's like all along there was this Amazon warrior locked up inside of her, and now she has an excuse to bring it out.

But she was not a person who believed in dreams very much. "Well, okay," she said, "if we're done with the dreams, let's —"

"Rachel," Jake interrupted, "I think I have something that may be interesting." He pulled a videocassette out of his bag.

"Cool. Let's watch a movie," Marco said.

"Not a movie," Jake said. "I guess no one else watched the late news last night?"

"I was busy watching my taped reruns of *Mister Rogers' Neighborhood*," Marco said, giving Rachel a sly look. "Last night it was the one where it was a beautiful day in the neighborhood."

Jake rolled his eyes up to the ceiling, the way he'd done a million times before when Marco said something irrelevant or annoying. "Rachel, can we go downstairs and use your VCR?"

"Sure," Rachel said.

We trooped down the stairs. Except for Tobias, who fluttered down above our heads.

"Hey, Tobias," Marco said, "I've been meaning to ask you, are hawks like seagulls? I mean, do they poop while they're flying?"

<Depends on who's down below,> Tobias shot

18

back. <Let me just put it this way — if you get on my nerves, you'd better buy a hat.>

Down in Rachel's living room, Jake turned on the TV and popped in his cassette.

"There was just this one small story," he narrated, as, on the screen, an old guy in a bathing suit held up a piece of what looked like metal.

"So now we're interested in hairy old guys who should be wearing shirts?" Marco asked.

"This old guy says he found that on the beach. It washed up during the storm a couple of days ago. Watch."

The camera focused on what looked like a jagged piece of metal, about two feet long and one foot wide. As the camera zoomed in, I saw what looked like letters. Only they weren't any alphabet I had ever seen.

Now the tape was showing the anchorwoman smiling, and then it went blank. Jake turned the VCR off.

"Okay . . . so?" Marco prodded.

Jake sighed. "So the night the Andalite landed, when I went inside his ship to get the cube that gave us our morphing powers, I saw writing."

I felt a chill creep up the back of my neck.

"I could be wrong, I mean, I'm not some expert," Jake said. "But I think it was that same alphabet. Those same kinds of letters."

Suddenly no one was laughing. Not even Marco.

"I think what washed up on the beach is a piece of an Andalite ship," Jake said.

Suddenly, without warning, I felt the ground swirl beneath me. I fell straight back, not even caring that Jake caught me in his arms just before I hit the carpet.

CHAPTER 4

I was falling, falling, falling.

Falling into the sea.

Splash! I hit the water. But still I fell. Down and down and down through blue-green, sunlit layers of water.

<I'm here,> a voice called to me. <I am here. I cannot survive much longer. If you hear me . . . come. If you hear me . . . come.>

Suddenly I opened my eyes. I stared up at Jake's concerned face.

Glancing across the room, I saw Rachel with the telephone to her ear, preparing to dial.

"She's awake!" Jake said.

"I'd better still call an ambulance," Rachel said.

"No!" Marco snapped. "Not unless we know she's hurt. It's too big a risk."

Rachel's eyes flared the way they do when someone tells her something she doesn't want to hear. "I'm calling nine-one-one," she said tersely.

"No, Rachel, I'm okay," I said. I sat up. My head felt a little woozy, but I was all right.

Rachel hesitated, her fingers just above the keypad. "What about Tobias?"

I looked around the room and saw Tobias spread out on the floor, one wing crumpled beneath him.

He looked dead.

I jumped up and ran to him.

"Rachel, Cassie seems okay, and nine-one-one can't help Tobias," Jake said.

Rachel replaced the receiver and ran over to Tobias.

"He's not dead," I said. I could feel him breathing. Then, just as suddenly as I had, he woke up. His enormous brown hawk's eyes opened, instantly fierce.

His first reaction was pure hawk. He hopped up and flared. Hawks flare just the way cats do when they're trying to intimidate someone. They hunch their shoulders and fluff up their feathers to make themselves look bigger than they are.

"Everybody stand still," I said quickly. "It's

okay, Tobias, you were just out for a minute there."

He quickly gained control over the hawk instincts. <That was strange,> he said.

"It happened to me, too," I said. "I passed out. And then I had the dream again. Only this time I could hear an actual voice. Or at least I heard thought-speech."

<Me, too,> Tobias confirmed.

"Okay, now this is getting weird," Rachel said. "Because at the same time I thought I kind of felt something."

"Yeah," Jake agreed. Marco nodded.

<I know this sounds crazy, but . . . but it's like someone is sending out a distress signal. Like they are calling for help.>

"Only this someone is in the water, or under the water, or something," I said. "Seeing that video, seeing that writing, it was like suddenly the message grew stronger."

"Or it may have just been a coincidence," Jake said. "This isn't a dream. I don't know what it is, but it isn't a dream. Even I halfway saw something. This is some kind of a communication."

"Well, this is all very interesting," Marco said, "but so what? I mean, are we getting some kind of psychic message from the Little Mermaid? What are we supposed to do about it?"

Jake looked closely at me. "Cassie? Was the voice in your dream a *human* voice?"

I was startled by the question. I hadn't really thought about it. I actually laughed. "When you asked me, the first thing that popped into my head was no, it isn't human." I laughed again. "But that doesn't make any sense."

<It's not human,> Tobias said suddenly. <I understand the meaning of what it's saying, but it's not human. It's not 'speaking' in words, really.>

"So what is it?" Rachel asked. "Yeerk?"

I let my mind drift back to the dream. I tried to hear the sound in my head again. "No, not Yeerk. It reminds me of something . . . of someone."

<The Andalite,> Tobias blurted.

I snapped my fingers. "Yes! That's it! It reminds me of the Andalite. When he first thought-spoke to us. That's what it's like."

"The Andalite," Marco muttered. He looked away. I knew he was remembering. We all were.

We had been walking home from the mall at night. Walking through a big abandoned construction site, when the Andalite ship had appeared above us.

It landed, and out came the Andalite prince, fatally wounded in a battle with the Yeerks somewhere in space.

He was the one who had warned us of the Yeerks — the parasite species that inhabited the brains of other creatures and enslaved them, making them Controllers. It was the Andalite who had warned us, and who, in desperation, had given us the great and terrible weapon — the power to morph.

We had been hiding, cringing in terror, when the Yeerks caught up with the Andalite. When Visser Three himself, the Yeerk leader, had murdered him.

I shuddered at the terrible memory of the Andalite's last, despairing cry.

"Yes," I whispered. "Tobias is right. It's an Andalite. That's who is calling to us from the sea. An Andalite."

For a few minutes no one said anything.

Then Rachel said, "He died trying to save us." She looked defiantly at Marco. "I know that doesn't mean anything to you. But the Andalite died trying to save Earth."

Marco nodded. "I know. And you're wrong, Rachel. That means plenty to me."

"Yeah? Well, if there's some Andalite calling for help, I'm going to try and help him," Rachel said.

I looked over at Jake and we shared this look, like "Oh, big surprise, Rachel is ready to go." I hid my smile and Jake kept a straight face.

"Tobias?" Jake asked. "What do you say?"

<I don't know if I should have a vote. I'm the one person here who isn't going to be much help dealing with water. Besides, you guys all know how I'd vote.>

Of all of us, it was Tobias who had stayed longest at the Andalite's side, even as the Andalite ordered him to get to safety. Something really deep had gone on between the Andalite prince and Tobias.

It was my turn. "I can't just ignore someone crying out for help, if that's what this is."

We all looked at Marco. I could see Rachel getting angry, like she was ready to jump all over Marco if, as usual, he disagreed.

Marco just grinned. "I really hate to do this. I really hate to disappoint you all." Then he grew serious. "But I was there at the construction site, same as all of you. I was there when Visser Three —" Suddenly his voice choked. "What I mean is, if there's an Andalite who needs anything, I'm there."

CHAPTER 5

"You do realize that if *we're* down here at the beach because of that news story, some *Controllers* are probably down here, too?" Marco asked for about the tenth time.

"Yes, Marco," Jake said patiently. "But maybe Cassie and Tobias can get some feeling from being down here, closer to the sea."

"So let me get this straight — we are now making decisions based on Tobias and Cassie's dreams, right?" Marco said. "And yet my dreams are totally ignored. The fact that I once dreamed about staying home and watching TV in total safety, that means nothing, right?"

"Right," Jake said flatly.

We were at the beach. The same beach where

27

the guy on the news had found what we now believed was a piece of an Andalite ship. It was night, with a sliver of moon that painted ripples of silver across the black water. A salt breeze blew off the water, making me feel peaceful and yet a little overwhelmed, intimidated, the way the ocean always makes me feel.

There is nothing as big as the ocean. It's like this entirely different planet, full of strange plants and fantastic animals. Valleys and mountains and caves and broad, flat plains, all hidden from our sight.

All I could see was the surface. All I could feel was the barest edge of the ocean, rushing over my toes as each wave crashed ashore.

But I could sense it out there. I could sense how vast it was, and how tiny I was.

"How about my dream of living long enough to get a driver's license?"

Jake gave Marco an exasperated look. "Marco, you can turn into a bird and fly. You could do it right now. Why would you care about driving a car a few years from now?"

"The babes," Marco said instantly. "Duh. You can't pick up girls when you're a bird." He glanced overhead, where we could see just the hint of dark wings against the canopy of stars. "No offense, Tobias. The wings are great, but I'm thinking of something bright red with about four hundred horsepower."

Marco's cooperative mood hadn't lasted long. I knew it wouldn't. Marco is never happy unless he's complaining about something. Just like Rachel is never happy unless she has something to fight against. And Tobias is never happy, period. He thinks if he's ever happy, someone will just come along and take his happiness away.

"So, Cassie?" Rachel said. "Do you *feel* anything?"

"Well, I feel a little embarrassed," I admitted. "And a little foolish."

"Maybe we could try calling the Psychic Friends," Marco suggested. "Hi, is this Psychic Friends? I've been dreaming about aliens lately —"

"Why Cassie and Tobias?" Rachel wondered aloud, ignoring Marco. "Why would they get these images so clearly and the rest of us barely felt anything?"

Jake shook his head. "I don't know. I mean, okay, say you're an Andalite. And you want to call for help. Who do you want to come and rescue you? Other Andalites, obviously."

"Tobias isn't an Andalite, and neither am I," I pointed out.

"I know," Jake said. "But maybe this communication, whatever it is, is tied into the ability to morph. You know, like morphing ability makes you able to 'hear' it. That way, only Andalites would be able to receive the call for help."

"Which still doesn't explain why Tobias and I —"

"Maybe it does," Marco interrupted, serious again. "Look, Tobias is permanently in morph. And Cassie, you're the one who has the most talent for morphing." Then he flashed white teeth in the dark. "Besides, you know you like animals more than humans, so it's like you're halfway into morph, anyway."

Suddenly a dark shape swooped low over our heads. <Lights!> Tobias said. <Up ahead on the beach. There's a bunch of people moving in a line with flashlights, like they're searching for something. You can't see them yet because they're hidden by that dune. But they'll be here in a couple of minutes.>

"Who are they?" Jake demanded.

<I can't tell,> Tobias said. <My eyes may be great during the day, but at night I don't see any better than you do. I'm a hawk, not an owl. Fortunately, I still hear pretty well. You guys hide in the dunes. I'll be right back.>

With that he was gone.

"Come on," Jake said. "He's right. Let's hide in the dunes."

We crouched down in a pocket between two dunes. I lay flat on my belly in the cold sand and peered through the tall sea grass, focusing on the bright line of the surf.

Tobias was back a few minutes later.

<It's them,> he said. He came to rest on a piece of driftwood. <It's a group from The Sharing. Chapman is with them.> He turned his head to look at Jake. <Tom is with them, too.>

The Sharing is a front organization for the Yeerks. Supposedly it's this group for all ages, like Girl Scouts or whatever. In reality it's a way for the Controllers to try and recruit new voluntary hosts. As impossible as it may seem, some humans actually *decide* to become hosts for the Yeerks. The Yeerks like it that way. It's easier for them to have a voluntary host instead of a host that resists their control.

The Sharing is very subtle, of course. People are brought along very slowly, over time. New members have no idea what it's all about at first. They think it's just fun and games.

I don't know when they tell the members what's really happening. By then I guess it's too late. They either become hosts voluntarily, or, like Jake's brother Tom, they are taken, anyway.

"Tom is with them?" Jake asked.

<I'm pretty sure,> Tobias said. <Some of the senior members — Chapman and Tom — are fol-

lowing behind the others. I could hear some of what they were saying. They're very worried about that fragment of Andalite ship.>

"So it *is* Andalite?" Rachel asked, excited.

<I guess so,> Tobias said. <I heard something else, too.>

The way he hesitated made me tense up. "What?"

<Something about Visser Three having visions. That's what they said. Visions. I guess the visions made the Visser cranky. He was on the mother ship at the time and decided to shove a Hork-Bajir out of an airlock because he broke the Visser's concentration.>

"It's because of Visser Three's Andalite body," Marco said.

"That's the connection. These dreams or visions or whatever they are must be some kind of communication that's only supposed to be heard by Andalites."

Suddenly I saw the line of flashlights swing into view. There must have been twenty people strung across the beach, all looking down at the sand, moving forward slowly.

"They're searching for any other fragments," I whispered.

A part of the line stopped moving. I heard someone yelling. Others came running up, excited.

"What did they find?" Jake wondered.

"I don't . . ." Then, in a flash, it came to me. "Our footprints! Four sets of fresh footprints that suddenly turn off into the dunes!"

"Let's get out of here," Jake hissed. "Now!"

Too late!

The flashlight beams raced across the rippling sand and up the side of the dune. In an instant a dozen flashlight beams focused on the notch where we crouched.

We slithered back, down and out of sight. Then we jumped up and ran.

"We should morph!" Rachel gasped as we stumbled over the sinking sand.

"No!" Marco said. "Tracks. We would leave tracks that went from human to animal."

"Get them!" someone yelled. Chapman, I think. He's our assistant principal at school. I knew his voice from hearing him yell in the hallways.

Jerky, wild beams of light danced all around us. We ducked and ran as fast as we could. But running across the sand was like running through quicksand.

Jake was gasping out whispered instructions. "Double around . . . if they follow us deeper into . . . the dunes . . . we can double around . . . get to the water . . . then morph . . ."

"There! There! I see them!"

A beam of light swept over me. I could see my shadow, long and twisted, projected on the sand.

I dodged left, out of the light. Just in time.

BAM! BAM!

Gunfire!

Someone was shooting at me.

CHAPTER 6

It seemed totally crazy.

I mean, I've been in one-on-one combat to the death with seven-foot-tall Hork-Bajir warriors, and I've been shot at by Dracon beams that sort of disintegrate you slowly. But I'd never been shot at with plain old everyday guns.

It seemed nuts after all we'd been through.

BAM! BAM! BAM!

Phit! I heard something hit the sand just inches from my foot.

"Aaaahhh!" I cried in surprise.

This was real. *Real!* This was really happening.

A rough hand grabbed me and dragged me

forward. Jake. I had frozen when I'd heard the bullet so close.

<They're all in the dunes!> Tobias cried. <Now's the time.>

"Come on!" Jake snapped. He half dragged me up the side of the nearest dune, but by then I was moving fine all on my own. I was scurrying up the side of that hill, snatching at handholds of scrub grass, pistoning my feet into the sand.

Over the top. We slid and rolled and ran down the far side.

We were back on the beach. I stole a quick glance to the right. No lights on the beach. They were all in the dunes. Looking for us.

"Head to the water," Jake said. "Morph to fish."

"Jake," I panted. "Trout . . . they're fresh-water fish . . . this is saltwater."

"You have a better idea?" he asked.

BAM! BAM!

"No," I said. We splashed into the boiling surf. As I ran I pictured the fish. I remembered being the fish. I focused as much as anyone can focus with a dozen or so Controllers chasing her and shooting.

My feet went out from under me. They had shriveled and begun to disappear. I hit the water and got a mouthful of salty foam.

I tried to keep my head above water, but my

arms were rapidly disappearing. The waves were high around me as I became smaller and smaller. My clothing billowed.

The people from The Sharing, the Controllers, raced to the water's edge. I could see their lights, weirdly distorted as my eyes went from the air-adapted eyes of a human to the eyes of a fish.

With what was left of my ears I heard, "The tracks lead right to the water."

Tom's voice. Then Chapman's. "I don't see them. They can't swim far. The current is too strong. Fan out up and down the beach."

"Do you think these are the Andalite guerillas?"

"No. The tracks are human. Just some kids, probably. I doubt they saw anything. That fool should not have been shooting."

"Sir," a new voice said. "We found a pair of jeans in the surf. Look like they could be for a kid."

"Any identification in them?"

"No. Nothing."

"Coincidence," Chapman said. "Probably."

"If they're human, why don't we see them out there?" Tom asked. "Four sets of human tracks. No humans in the water. Is it possible . . . is Visser Three wrong? What if they're not Andalites at all?"

I sank beneath the water. The morph was almost complete. But as I went under I heard Chapman laugh cruelly. "Visser Three wrong? Maybe. But I'm not the fool who's going to try and tell him."

The morph was complete. I was a fish, less than a foot long. A trout, to be exact. Excellent broiled, fried, or grilled.

The saltwater was harsh on my scales, and my gills were barely able to breathe.

<Everyone okay?> It was Jake. Now that we had morphed we had the same thought-speech ability as Tobias.

<I'm okay,> I assured him. <But I can barely breathe. I think we'd better be quick.>

<I'm with Cassie,> Rachel said. <I feel like my scales are burning up. And my gills are on fire.>

<Keep the shore on your left and go full speed as long as you can stand it,> Jake advised.

<Marco? Are you with us?> I asked.

<Oh, sure. Where else would I be? What could possibly be more fun than running around the sand dunes getting shot at and then jumping into the ocean and turning into a trout, who, incidentally, can't live in saltwater? I wouldn't miss it for anything. *Now* can we go home and watch TV?>

CHAPTER 7

The next couple of days we didn't get together, except for passing each other in the hallways at school. We do have lives beyond being Animorphs, after all.

Rachel was busy with her gymnastics class. Plus she got to go to this ceremony where her mom received some award for being Lawyer of the Year. (And since this is Rachel we're talking about, going to an awards dinner meant major shopping for new *everything*.)

Jake had totally blown a test because he hadn't studied, so he had to do a paper as makeup work. And I was busy helping my dad out in the barn with the golden eagle who had almost been electrocuted. He was at a difficult stage of his recovery.

Tobias dropped by one evening and acted kind of snippy about me trying to save a golden eagle. Golden eagles and hawks don't get along. Probably because golden eagles are known to kill and eat hawks.

It was a couple of days later that Jake rode his bike over to my house. I didn't expect him, so I was dressed like even more of a slob than usual. Plus I reeked of various horrible things because I was mucking out the stables and cleaning the birdcages.

Typical guy. He had the totally bad timing to show up when I looked like Ms. Manure.

"Hey, Cassie," he said in his usual casual way, like nothing was going on.

"Hi, Jake. Did you come by to help me shovel manure?"

He grinned. He has a great smile. It appears kind of slowly, like it doesn't quite belong on his serious face. "I don't know. Did I?"

"Yes, you did," I told him. I handed him a shovel. "If I have to smell, so do you."

We worked a little bit, with no sound but the steel shovel blades scraping the concrete. I knew he had something to tell me. I can always tell. But I figured I'd let him get around to it whenever he was ready.

"So," he said at last.

"So?" I echoed.

"Look, um, I guess everyone is kind of waiting to see what you decide to do."

This surprised me. I stopped shoveling. "What? What do you mean?"

"I mean, we're waiting to see what you decide to do about this dream of yours."

I shrugged. "I don't know. Besides, it's not just my dream. Tobias has it, too. And all of you guys felt it a little, at least."

"Yeah, but Tobias figures he isn't going to be much help when . . . I mean, if we decide to do something. We're talking water, and Tobias can't morph. As for the rest of us, I don't know. Rachel and Marco were talking about whether it might have just been something they imagined, you know? Because you made it seem so real and all."

"What do you think, Jake?"

Jake stopped working and wiped his forehead with the back of his hand. He looked straight into my eyes. "Cassie, if you tell me it's real, it's real. I think you and Tobias are right. But Marco is having second thoughts." He raised one eyebrow, as if to say "You know Marco."

I felt a queasy, sick feeling. "You mean, I'm supposed to make some kind of a decision? Like I'm supposed to say what we do?"

"Cassie, you're the one with the dream. Only you can decide if it's real, and if it's real enough for us to try and do something about it."

"I don't *know* if it's real," I said. What was he asking me to do? Every time we had tried to get into it with the Yeerks, we had ended up barely escaping with our lives. Just two days had passed since I'd heard bullets whizzing past me.

Jake waited until I met his gaze again. "Cassie, you know we all trust your instincts. You're the best at understanding animals. You're the best morpher. You know everyone in the group respects you."

I made a face. "Give me a break."

"If you think we should pursue this, you know Rachel will be right behind you. Me, too."

"And Marco?"

Jake grinned again. "Marco won't be right behind you. He'll be several feet back."

We both laughed.

"I don't know, Jake. It's a dream. It's like a vision or something. How do I know if it's real?"

He shook his head. "I don't know, Cassie. I guess you just have to take your best shot and hope you're right."

I cringed at that. I'm not Rachel. I'm not a risk-taker. "Can't you decide for me?" I asked, joking.

He nodded solemnly. "If you want me to, sure."

"And then if it's a disaster, it will all be on your head," I said. "You'll be the one who feels bad. You'll be the one to blame." I reached out and touched his cheek. "That's incredibly sweet of you. But you're right. I guess it's my decision this time."

I sighed and looked around at the barn. It smelled pretty bad, and sometimes it was a nuthouse of yammering birds and howling wolves and whinnying horses, all needing care, and all scared of the care we gave them. But it was the place I felt most at home in the whole world.

Out through the door of the barn, the fields of corn and open meadow stretched off into the distance, till they pressed up against the dark trees of the forest.

"I know this is crazy," I said, "but the ocean scares me a little. I understand the land. I understand soil and things that grow out of it." I laughed. "I guess I'm just an old farm girl. You know this farm has been in my family since the Civil War?"

Jake winked. "Do I know that? Puh-leeze. I had Thanksgiving with your family last year, you may remember. Your great-grandmother gave me the complete history."

"Going all the way back to when dinosaurs ruled the earth," I said. "Grammy does tend to go on about our history, doesn't she?"

He looked serious again, almost hard. "It's your call, Cassie. It will be really dangerous and we probably won't do much good. I mean, it's a big ocean out there. But it's your decision."

"Yep," I agreed. I shook my head slowly, sadly. "I believe these dreams are real. I believe there's an Andalite out there, somewhere . . . somehow . . . trapped. Calling for help."

"Good enough," he said. "Now. How do we get out there?"

I frowned, thinking of the possibilities. "Some kind of fish? It would have to be something fast. Something that isn't prey. You know, not some fish that's going to get snapped up by a hungry tuna or whatever."

Jake nodded. "And it has to be something we can acquire. Which means, probably, something at The Gardens."

"They have sea lions. And dolphins. But we can't morph them, can we?"

"Why not?"

"I . . . I don't know. It's just that, I mean, dolphins? They're highly intelligent. It seems kind of, I don't know, kind of wrong."

"Well, you decide," he said, leaning his

shovel against a wall. "I have to go. I can't blow another test, and I have to study."

He climbed back on his bike.

"You're just saying that to get out of shoveling manure," I said.

"Cassie," he said, "I would rather shovel manure with you than do homework without you, any day."

I think it was a compliment. Sort of.

He rode off, leaving me much less at ease than I had been before he'd come.

CHAPTER 8

The next day after school, the four of us headed toward The Gardens on a city bus. Tobias flew. He said he'd be there before we were, but he wasn't sure how close to *us* he actually could get.

The Gardens is this big amusement park that also includes a zoo. Only they don't call it a zoo, they call it a "wildlife park." My mom works there. Actually, she's the head of medical services, the head vet.

I have a pass to get in anytime I want, but the others all have to pay, which is kind of a drag because Marco never has any money. Ever since Marco's mom died, his dad has been kind of messed up. He just takes temporary jobs, and they're always broke.

I guess I kind of think it's romantic, the way Marco's dad has never gotten over his wife dying. But on the other hand, it's like I had to learn when I started helping my dad with the animals — sometimes death just happens, and all you can do is get over it the best you can.

It's tough for Marco because he feels like he has to take care of his dad — instead of having his dad taking care of him.

On the bus, I glanced over at Marco. He was looking out of the window, being kind of quiet.

"Hey, Marco," I said.

"What?"

"Is that a new haircut? It looks good."

"Yeah?" He looked surprised. He ran his fingers back through his long brown hair and kind of smiled.

I did some homework on the bus (math, gag, yuck!) and listened to my Walkman.

When we got there, it turned out there was a special on tickets — buy two and get the third ticket for a dollar. Marco had a dollar, fortunately, so we didn't have to go through any big scenes.

We cruised through the area where all the rides were, heading toward the wildlife park.

Jake shook his head sadly, looking up at the monster roller coaster. "That used to be the coolest thing in the world to me," he said. "But ever since I morphed a falcon, it just hasn't seemed like any big deal. I mean, you're going maybe eighty miles per hour on a steel track. When I was a falcon I did like two hundred miles an hour in midair."

"This morphing stuff does kind of change things," Marco agreed. "I used to want to get all pumped up. Then I morphed into a gorilla, and it was like, why bother lifting weights? I can just become a gorilla and bench press a truck."

"I don't feel that way," Rachel said. "Being a cat made me more interested in gymnastics. I mean, as a cat I was just so totally, totally in control and graceful. Ever since then I've been trying to use that feeling. When I'm on the balance beam I try and remember that cat confidence."

"And then you fall off just the same as always?" I teased.

"Oh, yeah," Rachel said with a laugh. She made little walking fingers in the air that then fell over. "Boom. I slip right off. But I feel *confident* while I'm falling off."

We reached the wildlife park entrance. The marine mammals are one of the first exhibits. There's a main building, then there are several outdoor tanks.

We went straight for the largest outdoor tank. There were bleachers all around it on three sides where people sat for performances. A show had just ended, and hundreds of people were leaving. The next show would be in a couple of hours.

"Good timing," Jake said. "Not too big a crowd."

"It's a weekday afternoon," I said. "It's never all that crowded on school days."

We forced our way upstream against the rush of people, and reached the side of the tank.

It's pretty big. Like four or five big swimming pools. It's very blue, very clean-looking. There's a low platform on one side where the trainers stand to communicate with the dolphins.

"So what's the difference between porpoises and dolphins?" Marco asked. "Both just fish, right?"

SPLOOSH!

The placid surface of the water exploded a few feet from us. Water sprayed across me.

"Oooooh!" we all said as one.

He flew straight up out of the water, like a sleek, pale gray torpedo. Eleven feet long from nose to tail. Four hundred pounds. He simply flew into the air, seemed to hang there, ten feet above the surface of the water, took a skeptical look at us, gave us his permanent wise-guy grin,

49

and slid back beneath the water so smoothly that there was barely a ripple.

"That is a dolphin," I said to Marco.

"Okay, I like that. *That* is excellent," Marco said. "Did you see what he did?"

You know how really great athletes never look like they're even trying? Like Michael Jordan? How everything they do is perfect, and you know they must have practiced for a million hours, but they always look like, "Oh. No big deal. Of course I can fly through the air. Nothing to it."

That's a dolphin in the water. Effortless. Perfect. Utterly in control.

Fish swim through the water. Sharks swim, tuna swim, trout swim, even people swim. Dolphins don't just swim through the water. They own the water. The water is their toy. The water is one big trampoline and the dolphins bounce around like kids having a good time.

Just watching them makes you happy. It also makes you feel like you're just this clunky, awkward windup toy, jerky and stumbling and clumsy. Human beings may be the smartest creatures on Earth, but we sure are dorky compared to a lot of other species.

"He's trying to get me to give him some more fish."

We all spun around. It was one of the dolphin trainers, a woman named Eileen.

"Oh, hi, Eileen," I said.

She nodded toward the dolphin, who was just exploding out of the water again. This time he turned a neat little somersault. "Joey is the biggest con artist. He's always trying to get extra fish."

"He's amazing," I said.

"Yes, he is," Eileen agreed, with a look of pride.

I introduced Jake, Marco, and Rachel. "We were looking at some dolphin information on the Internet," I lied, "so we thought we'd come out and see the real thing."

"Well, as you know, we have six dolphins here. Joey, whom you've met, Ross, Monica, Chandler, Phoebe, and Rachel. Hey, you guys want to feed them a little? You start throwing fish in the water and they'll all come over."

"It won't upset their schedule?"

"Nah. Just don't let Joey get it all. He's kind of pushy."

Eileen left us with a nice big bucket of fish.

"*That* is some nasty-looking fish," Marco commented.

"Once you morph into one of these dolphins, you won't think that," Rachel pointed out.

Marco gave her a skeptical look. "Do you realize that just a couple days ago we *were* fish? Not that much different than *these* fish?"

He was right. But it wasn't something I wanted to think about. I've always been very involved with animals. But it is a whole different thing when you can *become* different animals.

I took a fish by the tail and tossed it into the water. Just as Eileen suggested, the rest of the dolphins showed up very quickly.

"Wow. Think these guys like to eat?" Rachel asked.

The dolphins put on quite a show. They obviously knew how to impress humans.

"It's just weird the way they grin at you," Marco commented. "I mean, it's like they actually think something's funny."

"And they make eye contact," Jake pointed out. "They look right at you, right in the eye. Most animals seem like they're looking past you, or just looking to see what you are. These guys look at you like maybe they recognize you from somewhere."

Jake leaned over the edge of the tank to stroke one of the dolphins. "Hi there. Do I know you from somewhere? Jake's my name."

The dolphin tossed his head back and forth like he was nodding "yes," chattering in his high-pitched dolphin voice.

"Okay, now that was weird," Rachel said. "It was like he was answering Jake."

"Are you so sure he wasn't?" I asked. "Dolphins are very intelligent. Not our kind of intelligence, but still, I guess they're one of the two or three smartest animals around."

"It will be strange morphing something so intelligent," Rachel said.

"Yes," I agreed. Strange, and . . . wrong, somehow. I felt a twisting in my stomach. "How is doing this any different than what the Yeerks do?"

Rachel looked surprised. "Yeerks take over humans," she said. "Besides, they don't *morph*, they infest. We don't take over the actual animal, we just copy his DNA pattern, create a totally new animal, and then —"

"And then *control* the new animal," I said.

"It's not the same," Rachel insisted. But she looked troubled.

"It's something I'll have to think about," I said. "It's kind of been bothering me."

Jake joined Rachel and me. "We'd better do it."

I nodded. "Yes, we should, before we run out of fish to feed these guys." I leaned over the side of the tank and patted the head of the nearest dolphin. Her skin was rubbery, but not at all slimy. Just like a wet rubber ball.

She grinned up at me, fixing me with one eye as she cocked her head to see me.

I pushed away my doubts, closed my eyes, and concentrated on the dolphin. She became peaceful and calm, as animals always do during the acquiring process.

May I? I asked her silently. But of course she couldn't answer. . . .

CHAPTER 9

That night I dreamed again of the voice under the sea, calling for help. Only this time it sounded faint. Like a radio with the batteries growing weak. I wasn't sure if it was just a regular dream this time. A dream of a memory that might or might not be real.

And I dreamed of the dolphin in her tank at the wildlife park. The one they called Monica, although who knew if she had a true name of her own? How long had she been in that tank? How long since she had been free in the open sea?

The next day was Friday. There was no school because of some teacher conference, so we had a three-day weekend ahead of us.

I called Jake. "Hi, Jake. Are we going to the beach today like we planned?"

We were always very careful about anything we said over the telephone. Phone lines can be tapped. Besides, Tom, Jake's brother, could listen in on an extension and overhear something we didn't want him to hear.

"Actually, I was thinking the beach will be really crowded today," Jake said, sounding very casual. "I was talking to Marco and he said maybe we should go down to the river instead."

It was a good suggestion. We couldn't exactly morph on a beach full of people.

"I'll be there in two hours, okay? I have some chores to do."

I ended up being a little late. They were all waiting for me.

It was an area I had been to before with my dad. It's a little park near a bridge. A good place for fishing. About half a mile away, the river empties into the ocean. The river is lined with trees along most of its length. Here and there are homes and private docks, but the spot we'd chosen was hidden from the bridge and from any houses.

"Hi, Cassie," Jake said, smiling at me.

"Hi, everyone," I said. I spotted a movement in one of the tree branches. "Hey up there, Tobias. How's it going?"

<The same old thing. You know how it is. It's a hawk-eat-mouse world out there.>

I laughed, pleased to hear that Tobias was learning to be at peace with the fact that, at least for a while, he was as much a hawk as he was a boy.

<I'm going to be the timekeeper, watching the deadly two-hour limit,> Tobias said. <I'm the only bird in the world with his own watch.>

I looked closer and saw a very small digital timer strapped to one of his legs.

<Rachel put it on for me,> he explained. <I'll be over water the whole time, so I figured it was fairly safe. No bird watchers around to see me and wonder 'Hmmm, when did red-tails start wearing Timexes?'>

Jake said, "I figured we'd hide our clothes, then wade into the river a little way, then start morphing."

"Sounds good," Rachel said.

"Cassie? Will you go first?" Jake asked.

I nodded. "Sure." For some reason everyone has decided that I am the best morpher. I think it's mostly silly. We can all morph fine.

But the first time we morph a new animal it's always kind of tense. You never know what it's going to be like. You never know how much the animal's instincts and mind will resist you.

And this time there was a new fear, at least

57

for me. What sort of mind would I find? Would it be just the dolphin instincts, or would I encounter a true dolphin mind, with thoughts and ideas of its own?

I shed my overalls and kicked off my shoes, leaving just the leotard that I thought of as my morphing outfit. See, it's possible to morph some clothing along with you, but only something skintight. Anything bulky you try to morph just ends up as rags. And shoes? Forget shoes. We've all tried morphing shoes and it never works.

I stepped into the water. "Cold," I reported. The current tugged at my ankles.

I waded in a little farther, up to my waist.

Then I focused on the dolphin that was now a part of me.

The first change was my skin. It lightened from brown to pale gray. It was like rubber, tough but springy.

That was good. I wanted to hang on to my legs as long as I could. I wanted to change as many other aspects as I could before I had to drop down into the water.

I felt the odd crunching sound you get sometimes when bones are stretched or compressed. And right before my eyes — literally — my face bulged out and out and out still farther.

"Oh, man, that's definitely *not* attractive,"

Marco groaned from the shore. "Not a good look for you, Cassie."

Morphing isn't usually very pretty. In fact, it's the kind of thing that, if you didn't know it was going to be all right, would freak you out. I mean, I've watched while Rachel does her elephant morph, and I can tell you, it is the creepiest, scariest, most disgusting thing you'll ever want to see. Let alone watching people go from human to fish. Truly gross.

I didn't have a mirror, but I could guess how gross I looked. I had this huge, long bottlenose sticking out of my otherwise normal face. My skin was gray rubber. And when I felt behind me with my rapidly shriveling hands, I could feel the triangular blade of a dorsal fin rising out of my spine.

My arms were gone, replaced by two flat flippers, and I was now standing about ten feet tall, wobbling on my puny human-sized legs.

It was time to let the rest of the morph proceed. I surrendered my human legs. Instantly I fell face forward into the water.

I looked down and saw my tail. I was complete. The water was too shallow, though, and I was barely afloat. I kicked my tail, scraped across the sandy bottom, and finally surged out into deeper water.

I waited for the moment when the dolphin brain would surface, full of instinct-driven need and hunger and fear. The way it had always been before.

But it wasn't like that. It wasn't like a squirrel or even a horse.

This mind was not filled with fear and need.

This mind was . . . I know this sounds strange, but it was like a little kid. I tried to listen to it, to understand its needs and wants. To prepare myself for a sudden onslaught of crude, primitive animal demands. Flee! Fight! Eat!

But that didn't happen. I felt hunger, yes. But not the screaming, obsessive need that Jake felt when he morphed a lizard or when Rachel became a shrew.

There was no fear. None.

And fortunately, I did not find a true thinking, conscious mind. I breathed a sigh of relief. Just — again, I know it sounds strange — but I just found this feeling, like she wanted to play. Like a little kid who wants to play. I wanted to chase fish, catch them, and eat them, but that would be a game. I wanted to race across the surface of the sea, and that would be a game, too.

<Cassie?> I heard Tobias's thought-speech in my head. <Are you okay?>

Was I okay? I asked myself. <Yes, Tobias.

I'm . . . happy. I feel like . . . like I don't know. Like I want you to come and play with me.>

<Play with you? Mmmm, I don't think so, Cassie. Hawks don't do water.>

<Come on, everyone!> I called to the others. <Come on! Let's go! Let's swim to the ocean! I want to play!>

CHAPTER 10

<Let's go! Come on, you guys, let's go!>

I didn't like the river. I wanted the ocean. I could feel it close by. I could feel it in the way the current rushed me forward. I could feel it in some deep, hidden part of my dolphin being.

The ocean. I wanted it. It was my place. It was where I should be.

We swam in a school, the four of us, with Tobias flying overhead.

We raced the river's current, and soon I could taste the salt. I could feel the saltwater on my skin. It was as if I had opened the door of a toy store with every toy on Earth, and I had all the time in the world to play.

I saw my friends around me, swift, pale

shapes in the water. Sleek gray torpedoes as they rose to breathe.

I lived in both worlds — the sea and the air. I saw the blue-green of the ocean, the pale blue and white of the sky. I slipped back and forth through the bright barrier that separated them.

Jake went zipping by, shooting up from beneath me to explode into the air. I heard the slap of his belly as he landed. It was a game! I dove deep, down to where the sandy floor sloped toward depths even I could not explore. Then I powered my tail, steadied my flippers, and drove hard toward the surface. Above me I could see the shimmering, silver border between water and air.

Faster! Faster! I was a missile.

<Yah haaaaah!>

I shattered the barrier of the sea and hurtled up into the sky. I felt warm wind on my skin, instead of cold water. I hung, poised in midair, almost floating above the surface of the water. Now the barrier was beneath me. I pointed my nose toward it and dropped from the sky.

<Aaaaah!>

The water wrapped around me, welcoming me back.

<Is this cool, or what?> Marco laughed in my head.

<This is cool,> I answered.

<This is beyond cool,> Rachel chimed in.

<Let's all do it at the same time!> Jake said.

The four of us dove deep. The ocean floor was still far below us, rippling sand dotted with rocks and clumps of seaweed.

Near the ocean floor we leveled off, practically scraping our bellies on the bottom. And then, aiming at the silver barrier once again, we shot upward, racing each other, ecstatic from the joy of our own bodies' strength.

We launched into the air like a well-trained team of acrobats.

We flew, side by side, exhaling and refilling our lungs with warm air.

Life was joy. Life was a game. I wanted to dance. I wanted to dance through the sea.

So I did.

There was nothing I could not do. There was nothing I could ask of my body that it would not give me. Racing, spinning, turning, diving, skimming the surface, flying up into the sky.

I wasn't just *in* the sea. I *was* the sea.

<Are you guys just going to play all day?> It was Tobias. <You realize you've wasted forty-five minutes already?>

Minutes? I laughed. Who cared about minutes?

<Look, guys? I know you think the dolphin

mind hasn't affected you, but it has. You need to get a grip. You have a reason for being here.>

Reason? What was that?

<You're supposed to be looking for . . . well, for something,> Tobias said. <Something un-usual. An Andalite spaceship or something.>

Yes, he was right. He was definitely right. But would it be fun? Would it be a game?

<Find the spaceship. Cool,> Rachel said. <I bet I can find it first!>

<No way!> Jake said instantly. <I'll find it.>

<Where is it? Let's go look!> Marco said.

<Good grief,> Tobias said. <You're like a bunch of five-year-olds.>

But I was too distracted to care. <Hey. Can you guys do this?> I concentrated, and suddenly, from someplace in my forehead, came a series of loud, very rapid clicks, almost like loud static.

<Whoa! What was that?>

Then, to my total surprise, I heard something in those clicks. It was weird. It was kind of like hearing, only not. The clicking noises had hit something, far off in deeper water. I sort of *felt* the sounds as they came back to me, like scat-tered echoes.

There was a universe of information in that echo. Some of that information made me uneasy.

<You guys?> I said. <I know this is crazy, but

I feel like there's something out there. Something . . . I don't know. But I don't like it.>

The others immediately began firing off the clicking noise that is the dolphin's underwater radar. It's called echolocation.

<Yeah,> Marco said. <Now I see it. I mean, I don't see it, but you know what I mean.>

I searched in my dolphin mind, deep down in the places where instinct had been hidden beneath layers of intelligence.

Then a picture just popped into my consciousness.

<I know!> I cried, as if I had just won a contest. <It's a shark!>

Suddenly we weren't playing anymore. The others had all found the same instinct in themselves. The echolocation indicated that there was a large shark nearby.

And we knew one thing for sure. We didn't like sharks.

CHAPTER 11

<You know, I hate to sound like the only sensible person — so to speak — > Tobias said, <but you aren't here to fight sharks!>

<He's right,> I agreed. <Dolphins don't attack sharks unless the sharks attack first.>

<Wait . . . I'm getting more echoes,> Rachel interrupted. <There's more than one shark. And there's something bigger, too.>

I reached out with my echolocation sense and "felt" the sea ahead of me. <You're right,> I said. <Several sharks. And a *great one.*>

<A what?> Tobias asked.

I was confused. What *did* I mean? The words *great one* had just popped into my mind. <I

mean there's a *whale*. A whale. Being attacked by sharks.>

<A great one being attacked?> Marco asked. He sounded upset. It was strange, because we were all upset. More than we should have been.

<You guys do what you want,> Rachel said. <I'm going in.>

<Oh, there's a big surprise,> Tobias said with weary affection.

The four of us lanced forward, faster than ever, toward the whale in distress.

<I see them,> Tobias reported from the sky above. <Straight ahead of you. Looks like four, maybe five sharks and a big — really, really big — whale. Did I mention big? Wow. Big.>

We were steaming through the water when I caught sight of my first shark. He was bigger than me, maybe twelve feet long, with faint vertical stripes.

He was too excited by the hunt to notice me. Until it was too late. With every bit of speed and power I could get from my tail, I rammed the tiger shark in his gill slits.

WHOOOOMP!

It was like hitting a brick wall. My beak was strong, but the shark was made of steel or something.

I fell back, dazed. But as I tried to collect myself I saw that a trail of blood was billowing from the shark's gills.

I swam beneath him, and then I saw the huge shape of the whale. He was a humpback, more than forty feet long. Each of his long, barnacle-encrusted flukes was bigger than me.

He was trying to surface to breathe, but sharks were attacking, tearing at the soft, vulnerable flesh of his mouth.

It made me angry. Very angry.

Suddenly, from the murky depths, Jake and Rachel zoomed upward, like missiles aimed at the sharks.

WHOOMP! Rachel hit her target.

Jake's shark twisted just in time. Jake scraped across the shark's sandpaper skin, and before he could get clear, the shark was after him.

<Jake! He's on your tail!>

<I got him!>

<Look out! Coming up on your left, Marco!>

They were as fast as we were, as maneuverable as we were, and the sharks had one terrifying advantage — they did not know fear.

<He's on me! He's on me!>

<Aaaaarrrrgggghh!>

<Marco!>

<I can't see! Where is he?>

<Cassie! Below you, look out! Look out!>

It was no longer a game. I had gone rushing into a fight full of confidence and determined to help the whale. But now I was in a war. The sharks were killing machines. They seemed to be nothing but armored skin and razor-sharp fins and wide jaws with row after row of serrated teeth.

The water was boiling with twisting, turning, speeding sharks and us dolphins, locked in a high-speed battle to the death.

It suddenly occurred to me that we might lose. We might be killed.

I might be killed.

The water was dark with blood, still billowing from the shark I had hammered.

Suddenly two of the sharks turned away. They just turned and swam away. At first, I didn't know why.

Then I saw that they were following the shark I had wounded.

They were following the trail of blood.

They were at the limits of my sight when they struck. They ripped into the injured shark with wild, uncontrolled fury.

The last shark turned from the battle and went after them. Robbed of his meal of whale meat, he would feast on his brother instead.

<Everyone okay?> Jake asked.

<I have some cuts, but I'm okay,> I said.

<Same here,> Rachel said. She sounded tired. I guess I did, too. I felt exhausted and drained. The fight had probably only lasted two minutes from beginning to end. But it had been a long two minutes.

<Marco?>

<I . . . I think I'm hurt,> he said.

I looked for him. He was drifting in the water, almost motionless, twenty yards away. We all swam over, crowding around him.

Then I saw the wound. I think I would have screamed, if I could have. His tail had almost been bitten off. It was hanging by a few jagged threads. It was useless.

We were miles out in the ocean. And Marco could not hope to swim back.

CHAPTER 12

<He's going to die if we don't do something,> Rachel cried.

<Cassie?> Jake asked. <What do we do?>

<I . . . I don't know!>

<Cassie, you're the closest thing we have to an animal expert,> Jake said urgently.

But I wasn't feeling at all like an expert. I was feeling like a fool. This was all my fault. It had been my decision to go ahead. I was the one.

<Aaaahhh,> Marco moaned. <Oh, man. That's a major ouchie. Ahh, ahh!>

<What's happening?> Tobias called down. <Marco sounds hurt.>

<He is,> Jake answered tersely.

<Oh, man, I don't want to die as some fish,> Marco cried. <I don't want to die out here. My mom drowned. I'm going to die just like she did. My dad . . .>

<Morph!> I yelled. <I think I know what to do. Morph back to human.>

<If he morphs to human, he'll just drown,> Rachel argued.

<No. Morphing uses DNA, right? The basic pattern of the animal. Marco morphs back to human. I don't think the injury will affect him, because it doesn't affect his human DNA. Then, as soon as he can, he morphs back to dolphin. The dolphin body was injured, but the dolphin DNA should be the same. He should be a healthy, normal dolphin again.>

<What if you're wrong?> Rachel asked bluntly.

<There's no other choice,> Jake said. <Marco? You have to morph back to human. We'll keep you from drowning.>

<Jake . . . buddy . . . You know I can't swim.>

<I know, Marco. But we'll take care of you.>

<Okay. Yeah, okay. Might as well die in my own body. Ahh. Ahhhh! Maybe it won't hurt as much. Maybe . . .>

He was drifting off. <He's losing blood,> I said. <He may pass out. Marco. Morph. Now!>

We formed a circle around him, the three of us, with Tobias drifting overhead and the big humpback resting alongside.

Then Marco began to change. Arms sprouted from his flippers. His face flattened down, with his wide, grinning dolphin mouth shortening to form Marco's own lips. His skin turned pink and his morphing suit appeared.

His shattered, injured tail split in two. Legs formed from the halves, toes appeared. Human toes. At the end of human legs.

<He did it!>

"Yeah, I did it. And now I'm drowning!"

<Here,> I said, swimming beside him. <Grab onto me.>

He wrapped his arms over my back, and I held him up to the air.

Then I noticed something strange. It was like the ocean floor was rising to meet me.

No. It was the humpback. He had dived beneath us, and was rising slowly, slowly to the surface.

<Look out! The whale!> Rachel yelled.

But at that moment the most incredible part of an incredible day happened.

My mind, human, dolphin, both minds, opened up like a flower opening to the sun.

And a silent, but somehow huge, voice filled

my head. It spoke no words. It simply filled every corner of my mind with a simple emotion.

Gratitude.

The whale was telling me that it was grateful. We had saved it. Now it would save our schoolmate.

<Back away,> I told Rachel and Jake. <It's okay.>

<Yeah,> Rachel agreed, sounding amazed. <I hear it, too. Or feel it. Or whatever.>

The humpback rose beneath a sputtering Marco. The broad leathery back lifted him up. And when I looked again, I saw Marco, sitting nervously on what could have been a small island, high and dry above the choppy waves.

Tobias fluttered down and rested beside him.

The whale called me to him.

Listen, little one, he commanded, in a silent voice that seemed to fill the universe.

I listened. I listened to his wordless voice in my head. I felt like it went on forever.

Tobias said later it was only ten minutes. But during that ten minutes, I was lost to the world. I was being shown a small part of the whale's thoughts.

He had lived eighty migrations. He had many mates, many mothers, who had died in their turn. His children traveled the oceans of the world.

He had survived many battles, traveled to the far southern ice and the far northern ice. He remembered the days when men hunted his kind from ships that belched smoke.

He remembered the songs of the many fathers who had gone before. As others would remember his song.

But in all he had seen and all he had known, he had never seen one of the little ones become a human.

Marco, I realized. He means Marco. And little ones? Is that what the whales call dolphins?

We are not truly . . . little ones.

No. You are something new in the sea. But not the only new thing.

I wasn't sure what he was telling me. He spoke only in feelings, in a sort of poetry of emotion, without words. Part of it was in song. Part of it I could only sense the same way I could sense echolocation.

Something new?

He showed me a picture, a memory. It was a broad, grassy plain, with trees and a small stream. All of it underwater. And across the grass ran an animal that was part deer, part scorpion, part almost human.

Where is it? I asked him in a language of squeaks and clicks and mind-to-mind feeling.

And he told me.

Suddenly I woke up. That's how it felt, anyway. The whale released me. It was like coming out of a dream.

<Are you okay?> Jake asked. <You were starting to worry us, but we had this feeling maybe the whale didn't want us to interfere.>

<I'm fine,> I said. <I'm beyond fine.>

<Marco's ready to try remorphing,> Jake reported.

<Uh-huh,> I said, still lost in images from a mind larger and older and so utterly strange.

<Guys? You have about twenty-five minutes,> Tobias reported. <And it's a long way back to shore.>

I heard Marco say something, but he was speaking normally now, not in thought-speak, so it was hard to make it out with my ears under the water.

I stuck my head up and saw him begin to resume his dolphin shape.

Halfway through, he slipped off the side of the whale and back into the water. His fins formed. His beak.

And his tail. Perfect and healthy and undamaged.

We headed for shore, tired but alive.

I felt strange, leaving the whale. But when we were a mile away, I heard his song — slow, mournful, haunting notes.

<Why didn't he sing more when we were with him?> Jake wondered.

I smiled inwardly. And of course, since I was a dolphin at the moment, I smiled outwardly, too.

<He doesn't sing for the little ones,> I explained. <He sings for the mothers.>

<What?> Marco asked.

<He sings for a mate.>

<Ahh. Cruising for chicks. Got it. I wonder if the big old guy even realizes that he helped save my life.>

<Marco, that big old guy realizes things you and I will never even be able to guess.>

CHAPTER 13

The next day I went to see Marco at his home.

He and his dad live in a garden apartment complex. One of the older ones, on the far side of the big neighborhood where Jake and Rachel both live. I'd only been over there a couple of times. I think Marco is kind of embarrassed because he doesn't have much money.

He used to live in a house just down the street from Jake. But that was when his mother was still alive, and before his father had a breakdown and quit his job.

I knocked on the door. From inside I heard Marco's voice. "Dad, there's someone at the door. Put on your bathrobe, okay?"

There was a delay, and then the door opened. Marco looked annoyed.

"Cassie. What are you doing here?"

"I wanted to talk to you."

"To me? What about?"

"About yesterday," I said.

He hesitated. "Look, I'm spending the day with my dad, okay? We're thinking maybe we'll . . . you know, do something together."

"That's good," I said. Over Marco's shoulder I could see his father. He was wearing a bathrobe and sitting on the couch. He was staring at the TV. That was normal for any dad, I guess, on a weekend morning. But I had the feeling that Marco's dad was always sitting right there in front of the TV.

"Look, Marco, I just want to talk for a minute. Can I come in?"

"No, no," he said hastily. He stepped outside onto the concrete breezeway. Down below us was a swimming pool. It was drained and closed. Leaves covered the bottom.

"Marco, I wanted to talk to you about yesterday."

"What about it?"

"You could have been killed. It would have been my fault. This whole mission was my idea. Jake asked me if we should do it and I said yes."

Marco rolled his eyes. "That's it? Look, it wasn't your fault. It's this whole thing we're doing, this whole Animorph thing. I mean, it's been dangerous right from the start. It's insanely dangerous. What else is new?"

I shrugged. "What's new, I guess, is that the other times it was always someone else's idea."

"Oh, I get it. You don't like responsibility?"

I winced. Was that it? Was I afraid of taking responsibility? "I don't want to get my friends killed."

"And let me assure you your friends don't want to get killed, either," Marco said with a laugh. "I am completely opposed to getting killed." He grew serious, even sad. "But you know what? Sometimes bad things happen. That's the way it is."

I leaned against the rail, looking down at the dismal empty pool. "I see things die all the time," I said. "Animals, I mean. Sometimes you can't save them. Sometimes we even have to put them down — end their suffering. But my dad makes those decisions. Not me. He's the vet. I'm just his assistant."

"Look, here I am, all alive," Marco said, tapping his chest. "Get over it. I didn't have to go. It was my choice."

"Were you scared?"

For a while he didn't answer. He just came over and leaned on the railing beside me. "I'm scared all the time now, Cassie," he said at last. "I'm scared to fight the Yeerks, and I'm scared of what will happen if I don't. I look at Tobias, and what happened to him scares me to death. What if I get stuck in morph someday? And most of all, I am scared of . . . of *him*."

I didn't have to ask who Marco meant by *him*. Visser Three.

"That first time, in the construction site, when he killed . . . when he murdered the Andalite." Marco made a twisted smile. "I see that in my head every day. And the Yeerk pool." He shook his head. "That's something I would like to forget, too."

"Yes," I agreed. "There has been a lot of fear."

"So was I afraid yesterday? Bet on it. I was scared plenty. It was like, man, it's not bad enough we have to fight Hork-Bajir and Taxxons and Visser Three, we also have to fight sharks? Sharks?" He laughed, and hearing him brought the laughter out of me.

We both just stood there and giggled like idiots for a few minutes. It was that laughter you get after something really tense has happened. Relief laughter. "We're still alive" laughter.

"Um, by the way, I was going to wait and tell

everyone at the same time," Marco said, "but I think we have a problem."

"What problem?"

"It was in the newspaper this morning — two stories. One is about this guy who is going to be looking for some supposedly lost treasure ship off the coast. The other was this story about some big marine biologist guy who has a ship and is going to be doing some underwater exploration off our coast."

"Yes? So?"

"So, all of a sudden our nearby ocean seems to be very interesting to people. Treasure hunters and an underwater exploration? At the same time?"

"Controllers?"

He nodded. "I think so. I think it's all a cover story to explain why two ships will be out there with lots of divers in the water. I think it's them, all right. And I think they're looking for the same thing you're looking for."

I felt weak. The image the whale had given me surfaced in my mind. And the faint cry in my dreams, the cry for help.

"I . . . I can't ask anyone to go out there again," I whispered. "This time we might not be so lucky."

Marco looked uncomfortable. "Cassie, you know how I feel about all this. I think we have to take care of ourselves first. And our own families." He glanced back at his apartment door. "On the other hand . . . I guess after what the Andalite did for us, I wouldn't feel like much of a human being if I didn't try to save whoever is out there."

"I don't *know* who's out there," I said. "I don't know if it's even real."

"But you think it's an Andalite."

"I think it is. But Marco, I don't *know*. If someone gets hurt . . . killed . . . just because I have these dreams — I can't make that kind of decision."

"Yes, but can you decide to do *nothing*? That's a decision, too."

I had to smile. "Marco, you know, for a guy who's always joking around and being annoying, you're awfully smart."

"Yeah, I know, but don't tell anyone. It would destroy my image."

I started to walk away.

"You know what was strange about yesterday?" Marco said.

"What?"

"The sharks. They were so totally deadly. I mean, we worry about Hork-Bajir and Taxxons and Visser Three. You kind of forget that right here on little old planet Earth there are creatures just as tough and dangerous. It would be funny if it wasn't some alien that ended up getting us, but some normal Earth creature."

I didn't think it was funny at all.

Marco grinned at my stone face. "Okay, not funny ha-ha. More like funny weird."

CHAPTER 14

"□kay," Jake said. "Here's what we know. Or at least, what we think we know."

We were all at Rachel's house again. It was a few hours after I had gone to see Marco. Tobias was perched on the windowsill. He didn't feel all that comfortable being inside for long. He liked the feel of the wind and the open air.

"First, we believe that somehow a surviving Andalite, or maybe more than one Andalite, is trapped out in the ocean."

"Hopefully Andalites can hold their breath for a really long time," Marco joked.

"Second, Cassie believes she can find this Andalite, thanks to the information from the whale."

Everyone kept a straight face for about ten seconds. Then, all at once, everyone cracked up.

"Information from a whale," Marco repeated, giggling.

<Have our lives gotten really weird, or is it just me?> Tobias asked.

"Weird? Weird?" Marco crowed. "The talking bird wants to know if getting information on the location of an alien from a whale, that you've just saved from sharks, by turning into dolphins . . . You're suggesting that's *weird*?"

Jake smiled. "Well, stay tuned. It just gets weirder. Cassie and I have been going over maps. She says the location we're looking for is pretty far out to sea. Too far for us to swim and still have any time left of our two-hour limit."

"Well, that's the ball game, isn't it?" Marco asked.

Jake nodded at Rachel. "I was talking to Rachel earlier and she has an idea."

Rachel stood up. She'd been lounging on the bed. "We hop a ride on a ship. First we morph into something like a seagull."

Marco groaned. "I hate plans that begin with the words 'first we morph.'"

"We morph into seagulls," I said, picking up the plan we'd worked out. "Then we fly out into the shipping channel. We land on a tanker or a container ship or something that's going the right

87

direction. We morph back to human, rest up, let the ship get us closer, then jump over the side, morph to dolphin and go the rest of the way."

"Oh, well, when you put it that way, it sounds so easy," Marco sneered. "How about if we just walk over to Chapman's house and tell him to call Visser Three to finish us off? It's so much easier, and the results will be the same."

Jake sighed. "It is dangerous and risky, and there are about a hundred things that could go wrong. Plus, as Marco has told us, we have reason to think that Controllers will be out there, searching for the same thing we're searching for."

"This idea just gets better and better," Marco said.

"Let's put it to a vote," Jake suggested.

"I'm in," Marco said instantly.

A split second behind him, Rachel said her usual "I'm in."

Everyone stared openmouthed at Marco.

"Just once I wanted to beat Rachel to it," he explained.

"Tobias?" Jake asked.

<I don't think I should vote. I have to sit this one out. I can't stay up that long with nowhere to set down. Sorry.>

"You had the dreams, just like Cassie," Jake

pointed out. "Do you think we should do this or not?"

Tobias fixed his fierce glare on me. <Yes, Cassie and I both had the dreams. I think they're real.>

"Okay, looks like we go," Jake said briskly. "Tomorrow. First thing in the morning. We can't wait any longer. The longer we hold off, the greater the chance the Yeerks will beat us to it."

We left Rachel's house. Marco split off in one direction. Tobias flew off to some unknown destination. Jake and I walked together for a while, even though it was out of his way.

"I think Tobias is feeling kind of left out," I said. "You should talk to him later, remind him of how many times he's helped us out."

"That's a good idea," Jake agreed.

We walked a little farther in silence. It's one of the nice things about the relationship Jake and I have. We can be quiet together and feel okay about it.

"This is really dangerous, isn't it?" I asked him.

He nodded.

Suddenly I stopped walking. I don't know why, but I had this need to tell him something. I took his hand and held it between both of mine. "Jake?" I said.

"Yes?"

It was on the tip of my tongue, but then it seemed ridiculous to say it. So instead I said, "Look, don't ever get hurt, okay?"

He smiled *that* smile. "Me? I'm indestructible."

The way he said it, I almost believed him. But then, as he went his way and I headed toward home, I glanced up at the sky.

Against the blaze of sunset I saw a flash of russet tailfeathers. Tobias. Our friend, who had been trapped forever in a body not his own.

None of us was indestructible.

CHAPTER 15

<Hey! Half a sandwich! It's salami!>

<Look over there. Is that a Jujubee?>

<Pizza! Pizza! Part of the crust and it's one of those stuffed crusts!>

Fortunately, one thing we always have plenty of in the Wildlife Rehabilitation Center (also known as my barn) is seagulls.

We acquired the seagull DNA. Then the four of us, with Tobias watching from the high rafters, morphed into the new bodies.

I have been a bird before. An osprey, to be exact, one of the types of hawk.

But gulls are different in some ways. For one thing, they are scavengers, not predators. So as we took wing and flew in a rush of white from the open hayloft, I noticed different things, felt different things. My seagull mind was not searching for mice or scurrying animals. It was much more openminded. My seagull intelligence looked for anything — *anything* — that could even possibly be food.

Fortunately, the gull brains were close enough to the other bird brains we'd all experienced that it was fairly easy to control them. We didn't waste a lot of time getting started.

Although, once we did get started, everyone was constantly pointing out food.

<Hey! Look! French fries on the ground.>

<Whoa! That's half a 3 Musketeers bar by that car!>

<Oooh, ooh! Look at the Dumpster behind that McDonald's!>

Sometimes you just have to accept the animal's basic mindset and go with it.

<There's the beach,> Jake said as we flapped and soared and flapped some more.

It's easier being an osprey in some ways. Much less flapping.

Once we were out over the water, we could at least stop scanning for food. Mostly.

<Hey! Is that a bag of potato chips floating down there?>

We flew low, just a few dozen feet above the

water. Not like hawks, who can ride the thermals up to the bellies of the clouds.

But Tobias wasn't much higher than we were now. There are no thermals over water and he was having to flap a lot to stay aloft.

We flew on, skimming the choppy surface of the water.

<Hey, look,> Rachel said. <Over to the left.>

Sleek gray shapes sliced through the water, up, down, up, down, breaking the silvery barrier between sky and sea. It was a school of dolphins.

<You know, sometimes this is just so wonderful,> Rachel said. <I mean, we're flying. We're flying! And later, we'll be like them, at home in the water.>

<Yeah, just us and the sharks,> Marco said darkly.

<Still, it *is* cool,> Rachel said.

<There's a ship up ahead,> Jake announced.

<You just now noticed it?> Tobias laughed. <Wow. Seagull eyes aren't exactly great, are they? It's a container ship called *Newmar*. It's from Monrovia. You want to know what color the captain's hair is?>

<Show-off,> Jake grumbled.

Hawk eyes are totally amazing. As long as it's sunny out, Tobias can read a book from like three blocks away.

It was hard, flying to catch up to the ship. It was moving fairly fast, and by the time we were close I was exhausted.

The ship was gigantic, painted a rusty blue, with a deck longer than a football field. The superstructure was all crammed toward the back. That's where the crew would be, so we flew forward, hoping to find someplace private.

The deck was stacked with containers, big steel boxes like trailers. Row after row of them lined the deck, and we could see hundreds more down in the hold.

We settled in the narrow space between two rows of containers, far forward. It was like having walls all around us. Corrugated metal walls that went high over our heads.

<Tobias? How much time?> Jake asked.

Tobias twisted his head down to see the tiny watch strapped to his talon. <It's been about an hour and a half.>

We decided to resume our human shapes. The space between the rows of containers was even narrower when we were fully human again.

"Brrr. It's chilly out here," I said. The steel deck was cold beneath my bare feet. And even though the sun was high in the sky, we were in shadow.

"Man, I swear, this is the worst thing about

morphing," Marco said. "Can someone please figure out how to morph shoes, and maybe a sweater? Come on, Cassie. You're the morphing genius. I'm sick of these morphing outfits."

"But you look so cute in Spandex," Rachel teased him.

"Plus, they aren't exactly fashionable. All I'm saying is — uniforms. Something cool-looking. And warm. Warm would be nice. When winter comes, we are going to be some sad little Animorphs."

"I have a more important question," Rachel said. "How do we know when we're there? You know, our destination."

Jake made a "who knows?" face. "I figure this ship is going like, what, twenty miles per hour? Figure an hour, and that puts us twenty miles out, right?"

Rachel pointed a finger at her forehead and said, "Jake's a total mathematical genius. One hour at twenty miles per hour. Right away he figures out that's twenty miles."

Jake laughed. "That's about all the math I can do."

<Actually, we're moving about eighteen miles per hour,> Tobias said.

We all just stared at him.

<I fly along the roads sometimes and watch

the car speedometers. So I have a pretty good idea how fast I'm flying. When we were flying alongside the ship, I clocked it.>

"Okay, eighteen miles an hour, more or less, straight south," Marco considered. "That would put us within a couple of miles of where Cassie thinks we should go."

I winced. Every time anyone said something about me deciding where to go or what to do, it made me nervous.

<I'd better head back,> Tobias said regretfully. <I don't want to try and fly eighteen miles back without a rest. And if I stay on this ship I'll end up in Singapore.>

"Singapore?" Rachel asked.

<Yeah. I read the captain's log as we were flying alongside. That's where they're heading.>

Tobias flew off, leaving us the little watch.

It was extremely dull waiting for an hour, with nothing to do but try and guess what was in the big containers all around us. On the other hand, we knew what we had to do next would definitely not be boring.

So basically, we were happy to just be bored for a while, huddling together to stay warm in the whipping ocean breeze.

After a long time, Jake checked the watch. "It's been about an hour. Cassie? What do you think?"

"I don't know," I admitted. "I . . . I guess I was hoping that when I was back in dolphin morph I would be able to make sense of more of the details the whale communicated to me. It was mostly images. And some of the images were about sounds and currents and water temperatures, and stuff you can't see from the surface."

Jake thought for a moment. "Oh, well, now is as good as any time, I guess. Let's head for the side."

We stood up, uncramping our cold, stiff legs and arms. We moved along the row of containers toward the left side of the ship. The port side, as they say.

We reached the side. There was a solid steel railing that ran all around, about waist high. Jake checked to see if we would be in view of the bridge, and we headed forward a little more to a blind spot where no one should see us.

The four of us leaned over the rail and looked down at the water. It looked like it was a million miles below.

Marco whistled. "Man. That is some high dive."

"No big deal for a seagull or a dolphin, but a mighty long way for a human," I agreed.

"We can't morph up here. We'd never get our dolphin bodies over the side," Rachel pointed out.

"Nope," Jake agreed. "We have to jump in with our human bodies. All except Marco. He can't swim. I thought he could morph up here, and then we could all shove him over the side."

Rachel looked skeptical. "Jake? When Marco is in dolphin morph, he'll weigh like four hundred pounds."

Jake looked worried. "I kind of didn't think about this when I was planning."

I had a sinking feeling. The plan was falling apart before it had even begun.

"I'll lean against the railing," Marco suggested. "I'll start morphing, then, before I lose my legs, you guys help shove me over. I'll finish morphing within a few seconds of hitting the water."

"Unless the water knocks you out and you just sink," I said flatly. "Forget it. Forget it. Let's just morph back to seagulls and fly back home. This is insane."

"Insane?" Marco echoed. "Hey, that's my word. Look, we came this far."

"I don't care!" I yelled, surprised at my own passion. "I'm not going to be responsible for anyone dying! This isn't going to work. I don't know where I am. I don't know where we're going. I don't know what to do!"

Marco laughed. "Excellent pep talk, Cassie. Now I'm *really* looking forward to this."

I was going to yell at him, something like, "Look, Marco, this is not a joke." But when I looked at him, I saw that his face was bulging way out, forming a long, grinning beak.

He had already started to morph.

"I'm nock koink to . . ." he started to say. But his mouth no longer worked.

He was growing larger, straining his weak human legs with his weight. His arms were flattening into flippers.

"Now!" Jake said. He grabbed Marco's flipper arm. Rachel and I jumped forward and seized his legs just as they began to shrivel.

"Heave!" Jake yelled.

Marco, half human, half dolphin, tumbled backward over the railing and fell into the sea.

"Let's go," Jake said.

"Yee-hah!" Rachel said with a wild grin. She jumped up on the railing, balanced for a moment like the gymnast she was, then launched herself off in a neat swan dive.

Jake and I exchanged a glance.

"Rachel," he said, and rolled his eyes.

"She's *your* cousin," I pointed out.

"On the count of three. One, two . . ."

"Ahhhhhhhhhhhhhh!" I climbed over the railing and launched myself as far from the steel wall of the ship as I could.

CHAPTER 16

"**A**aaaaaaaaaahhhh!"

I fell for what seemed like a very long time.

PAH-LOOOOSH!

I hit the water feet first and plowed beneath the surface in a pillar of bubbles.

The cold shocked me. The water was like ice. And just a few feet away was the intimidating steel wall of the tanker, sliding past at what felt like incredible speed.

I kicked my feet and began to rise to the surface. I've been a swimmer since I was little, but it frightened me, being this far out in water this deep. This wasn't a pool or a pond. This was the ocean. Twenty miles from land.

I broke the surface and gasped a lungful of air

and a mouthful of saltwater. What had looked like a little choppiness from up in the ship felt like towering waves down here. I couldn't see any of the others. All I could see was the side of the ship.

Come on, Cassie, I told myself, morph. Do it. This is no place for a person.

There is just about nothing as helpless as a human being in the ocean. Without my ability to morph I would not have lasted an hour.

I felt the change begin as I focused on morphing. At first, I thought it would kill me. I soon had most of the weight of a dolphin, with nothing but my human feet paddling to keep my head above water. My arms had already become flippers.

A wave washed over me, leaving me sputtering from my mouth and my blowhole at the same time.

I realized I could no longer keep my head above water. I took a deep lungful and let myself sink.

As my eyes went from human to dolphin, my underwater vision improved. I could see other figures kicking and writhing in the water around me. Jake, half-changed. Rachel, almost complete. Marco, with a dolphin grin, looking amused.

Then, with a kick of my newly completed tail, I knew I was safe. I had made the change. I was a dolphin in a dolphin's world. The human clumsiness, the human cold, the human fear of an alien environment, all evaporated.

I was warm and in control and right where I should be.

<Everyone okay?>

One by one they answered. We had made it. Too bad this was just the easy part of the mission.

<Well, that was fun,> Marco said sardonically. <Let's never, *ever* do it again.>

<Cassie?> Jake prodded me.

I tried to relax, to let my human mind recede just a little. I needed to listen to the dolphin instincts. I needed to understand the whale's instructions. Something no human could ever do.

<Not far,> I said. <We're just a few . . . um . . . Forget it, there's no word for it. Just believe me, we're close.>

<After you, Cassie,> Jake said.

It felt strange, taking the lead. But only I knew the way. We traveled near the surface for a while. This made it confusing for me, because whales go deeper, and the world the whale saw and knew was a deeper world than I, as a dolphin, experienced.

And yet, I knew I was going in the right direction. My echolocating clicks painted murky, half-understood pictures in my mind of underwater hills and valleys and rifts. I felt currents tugging at me. I sensed changes in water temperature.

In the end, I just knew.

<Okay, everyone, get a good lungful,> I said.

We surfaced, blew out the stale air, and filled our lungs with the good clean ocean air.

<Hey. What's that?> It was Rachel.

<What?> I asked her.

<Over there. It's a helicopter.>

We all watched as a helicopter flew low and very slowly over the water. It was just a few hundred yards away, and with our dolphin vision, we couldn't see it as well as we might have with our human eyes.

But as it flew closer, I could see that it was dragging a cable through the water.

<Some sort of sensor,> Jake speculated.

<They're looking for something in the water,> Marco agreed.

<It's them,> I said.

No one argued. We all knew it was true. Controllers were flying that helicopter.

The Yeerks were here.

CHAPTER 17

<Everyone take in as much air as you can,> I said again. <We're going deep.>

We dove and swam almost straight down. Down, down, leaving the bright barrier behind. Away from the sun. Away from the light. Away from the air that we needed just as much as humans did.

I echolocated a school of fish ahead, just below us. But we weren't there to eat lunch. We swam through the fish and still we headed down. Down until we could see the ocean floor beneath us.

We leveled off and skimmed across the ocean floor, like low-flying jets racing at treetop level. Over waving fields of seaweed. Through darting schools of fish. Over jutting extrusions of rock, encrusted by barnacles and home to a thousand bizarre crabs and lobsters and urchins and worms and snails.

Ahead was a ridge, a sort of long, low hill. We sailed over it.

<I'm starting to feel like maybe taking a breath would be a good thing,> Rachel said. <How much farther —>

We all saw it at the same time.

Saw it, yes, but could hardly believe it.

I've become used to seeing impossible things — aliens, spaceships, my own friends turning into animals. But this was just plain mind-boggling.

It was round. As round as a plate. A very large plate. From one side to the other, the diameter must have been half a mile.

It was covered by a transparent dome. Clear glass, or whatever it is the Andalites use for glass.

And within the dome, protected from the crushing force of the water, was what looked very much like a park.

A park, in a plastic dome, at the bottom of the ocean.

There was grass, more blue than green, but it still looked like grass. There were trees like huge stems of broccoli. And other trees like orange and blue asparagus spears. At the center was a small lake, crystal-clear blue water. From the water grew fantastic, transparent green crystals in shapes like eccentric snowflakes.

<Whoa,> Marco said.

<Man,> Jake commented.

<Is this what you expected, Cassie?> Rachel asked me.

<I . . . I had dreams . . . I saw flashes of something . . . but this! This is unbelievable.>

<I think that may be a hatch down there,> Marco said. <You see the part that sticks out?>

<Let's try it,> Jake said. <I can't hold my breath much longer.>

We arced down toward a part of the glass dome that seemed different from the rest. As we got closer, we could really begin to feel the size of the dome. It was like approaching one of those huge stadiums where they play football. But even bigger, if you can imagine that.

<It is a hatch,> Rachel reported. She was a little ahead of the rest of us. <It's some kind of a glass door. On the other side there's a little room, then another door that leads into the dome. There's a little red panel beside the outer door.>

<Let's either try it or surface,> Marco said urgently.

<That red panel. That's got to be the door-

knob,> Jake said. <Here goes. Let's hope this works.> He pressed his beak against the panel.

Instantly the outer door opened.

<We should try this one at a time, see if it's safe,> Marco said.

<Not enough time,> I said. My lungs were burning. I needed air.

The four of us swam in through the outer door. There was a second red panel. I punched it with my beak and the door closed, sealing us into a small, glass room. We could see out and up into the ocean all around. But the side leading into the dome was opaque.

<I knew we'd end up in an aquarium sooner or later,> Marco said.

The water began to drain from the room, slowly, a little at a time. This opened an area of air at the top of the enclosure. I raised my blow-hole and sucked in blessed oxygen.

<Okay, let's morph,> Jake said.

I had already started. By the time the enclosure was half drained, I could stand on my own human feet.

"We made it," Marco said after his human mouth reformed. "I don't know where we made it to, but we made it."

The enclosure was empty now. The four of us stood there barefoot, dressed only in our soggy morphing outfits. There was one last red panel beside the door leading into the dome.

"Ready?" Jake asked.

"As ready as I'll ever be," Marco said.

Jake pressed it with his hand.

The door slid open. I felt a wave of warm, incredibly fragrant air rush in.

I caught a glimpse of . . .

Then a brilliant flash of light . . .

And suddenly I was unconscious.

CHAPTER 18

I opened my eyes. I was staring straight up. I was on my back. Above me I could see the ocean all around. High overhead, fish swam by, sparkling. Higher still I could see the bright barrier between sea and sky. But it was very far away.

I rolled my head to the side. Jake was beside me, still unconscious. There was blue grass under my head. I looked the other way.

"Yaaaahh!"

<Do not move. I stunned you to see what you are. But if you move, I will destroy you.>

He stood on four delicate hooves, looking, at first glance, like a pale blue and tan deer or antelope.

But he had a strong upper body, like a mythical centaur, with two small arms and many-fingered hands. His face was almost triangular, built around two huge, almond-shaped eyes. There was a small vertical slit where his nose should have been, and nothing where his mouth should have been.

From atop his head rose twin horns. Only they were not horns. They each ended in an eye and turned this way and that, independent of his main eyes.

He seemed gentle, quizzical, almost delicate. Until you noticed the tail. The tail was like a scorpion's. It was thick, powerful, and ended in a wicked scythe blade that literally glittered along its razor-sharp edges.

I knew what he was. There is no mistaking an Andalite when you see one.

And there was no question about what he was holding in his hand, either. It looked a lot like a Yeerk Dracon beam.

He was pointing it at me.

The others were waking up all around me.

"What the . . . Oh," Marco said. "Please tell me that's a real Andalite and not Visser Three."

Suddenly, without warning, the Andalite's tail arched forward. The blade stopped inches from Marco's face.

<Visser Three! Do not speak that name!> the Andalite thought-spoke.

"O-o-o-o-kay," Marco said slowly. "Whatever you want."

"We are friends," I said.

<I don't know you,> the Andalite said. But he withdrew his tail and Marco started breathing again.

"You *called* me," I said. "We've come to help you."

<Called? You heard my call?> He fixed all four of his eyes on me. <What are you?>

"Human. A person of Earth."

<I have seen images of your kind. My call was to my cousins. How did you hear it?>

"I don't know," I admitted. "I heard it in my dreams. So did a friend of mine. We guessed it was an Andalite. We wanted to help."

<What do you know of Andalites? My people are not known to humans. You do not travel the stars. You know only your own planet. My elder cousins have taught me this.>

"We knew one Andalite. We were with him when . . . when he was killed."

The Andalite narrowed his main eyes. <Who was this Andalite you say was killed?>

I searched my memory for his name. He had told us, but it was a strange, long name. "I can't

111

remember all of his name. But part of it was Prince Elfangor."

The Andalite jerked as if he'd been hit. His entire body seemed to quiver. His deadly tail arched high in the air.

<Prince Elfangor? No one could kill Elfangor. He is the greatest warrior ever. No one could kill him!>

"Someone did," Jake said. "We were there."

<Who? Who do you claim killed Elfangor?>

"The one whose name you don't want us to speak," I said softly.

The Andalite held his head high, but his tail sagged and dragged down to the grass. He lowered his weapon. <He was my brother. Did . . . did he die well? In battle?>

Jake answered. "He died protecting us, and defying the Yeerks to the end. At the very last moment he struck with every weapon he had."

The Andalite closed his main eyes for a brief moment. <My brother was a great warrior. His cousins loved him. His enemies feared him. No more can be said of any Andalite warrior.>

I was surprised by what Jake said next. "I've lost a brother, too. He's one of *them*. A Controller."

The Andalite opened his eyes. <And you, human. Do you serve the Yeerks or fight them?>

"I fight them. We fight them."

112

<With what weapons? Do you have powerful weapons?>

"Only the weapon your brother gave us," I said. "The power to morph."

<Elfangor gave you that? It is never done!> He seemed disturbed. <The situation would have to be very bad for him to give you morphing capability.>

"The situation is worse than you think," Marco said. "The Yeerks seem to know you're here. Some piece of Andalite wreckage washed up on shore. They are up on the surface right now."

For the first time the Andalite seemed uncertain. <What is your plan?>

"To get you out of here and hide you," I said.
<You came only to rescue me? This is true?>
"Yes."

He smiled with his eyes, just as Prince Elfangor had done. <You will be tired after this last morph. You will need to rest.>

"A little while, yes," I agreed.

"What is this?" Rachel asked. "This dome, I mean. It's like a park or something."

<This is the main part of an Andalite dome ship. It is where we live. The engines and the war bridge are in a long section that sticks out from the bottom, with this dome perched on top.>

"Like a mushroom. Or an umbrella," I suggested.

The Andalite just looked blank.

"Never mind," I said.

<During the great battle in orbit over your planet, the dome was separated from the rest of the ship.>

"Why?"

The Andalite dug at the grass with his fore-hoof. <I . . . I was too young for battle, by the laws of our people. Besides, the rest of the ship maneuvers better without the dome.>

"You're a kid? I mean, like a young person?" Marco asked.

<Yes.>

"Are you the only one left? The only Andalite here?"

<Yes. I am alone. When the Blade ship appeared unexpectedly, they caught us off guard. I saw the main section burn. Dracon beams damaged the orbital stabilization of this dome. It fell. It splashed into the ocean and sank to the bottom. I have been here for these many weeks, hoping that my cousins would come for me. Hoping that some survived. Finally I risked sending out a mirrorwave call. It works by . . .> He stopped, and looked embarrassed. <I am not supposed to explain Andalite technology. My brother will . . . He would have been angry with me.>

"Just you survived," I said sadly.

<Just me,> he said. <No prince. No warriors.>

I felt a sinking in the pit of my stomach. I think the others felt the same way. I guess we'd all kind of been hoping this Andalite would be like the prince. A leader. Someone who could take over the battle. Someone who would know more than we did.

"We're young, too," I said. "Too young to fight, according to the laws of our people."

<But still you fight!>

"We feel like we don't have a choice. Look, we don't even know your name. This is Jake, Rachel, Marco. I'm Cassie. There's one more. His name is Tobias."

<I am Aximili-Esgarrouth-Isthil.>

We all just kind of stared.

"Ax," Marco said. "Pleased to meet you."

<Who is your prince?>

One by one we looked at Jake.

"Oh, give me a break," Jake said. "I am not anyone's prince."

But the Andalite had stepped forward. He bowed his head and lowered his tail. <I will fight for you, Prince Jake, until I can return to my cousins.>

CHAPTER 19

<This is a derrishoul tree,> Ax said. He pointed to one of the asparaguslike spears that grew straight and tall. He was showing us around while we recuperated from the morphing.

<And that we call enos ermarf.>

"What?" I didn't see what he was pointing at.

<That. The way the lake curves forward into the grass, framed by derrishoul trees.>

"You have a word for something like that?" I asked.

<There are names for all the many ways the water and sky and field interact,> he explained. <And for the way the suns and the moons hang in the sky of our planet, and cast their lights in one

116

way or another on the different aspects of the world.>

Rachel caught my eye and silently mouthed the words, "He's cute." Then she winked.

I wasn't sure I agreed. Andalites are halfway between looking cute and looking scary. You can get past the weird stalk eyes and the fact that they don't have mouths (at least not that you can see), but that scorpionlike tail is far from cute. It reminded me of the sharks.

"You all live here?" Marco wondered. "I mean, just out in the open? Out on the grass?"

<Where else would we live? Here we have space to run. There must always be space to run.>

"This is like actually being on another planet," Jake marveled. "This is all like part of the Andalite world."

<Yes. We take our home with us into space. It angers the Yeerks,> he added grimly.

"Why do they care what you take into space?" Marco asked.

<It is a part of everything they hate and would destroy if they could. The Yeerks would take our world and make it as barren as their own. As they will to your planet unless they are stopped.>

I grabbed Ax's arm. "What . . . what are you saying? What do you mean about making the planet barren?"

117

He turned his big eyes on me. <The usual Yeerk pattern. Once a planet is under their control, they alter it to suit their own desires. They will leave enough plant and animal species to keep the host bodies fed — humans in the case of Earth — and the rest they eliminate.>

He said it like it was obvious. Like it was just something I should know.

He started to move on, but I held his arm tightly. "Wait, wait. I don't think I understand you. What do you mean, they eliminate species?"

<They eliminate them. They will make Earth as much like the Yeerk home world as possible. They will destroy most of the plants and all of the animal species except those they eat.>

I let go of his arm. I rocked back and grabbed at the air for balance. I felt like I'd been hit by a car. "No," I whispered. "That can't be. You're just saying that because you don't like Yeerks."

The others were staring. No one was moving.

Ax looked around at us. His eyes narrowed. <Don't you know? Don't you know whom you're fighting?>

"We know they take over people's minds," Rachel said weakly.

<Yes. And that is one of their great crimes. But the Yeerks are more than that. Yeerks are killers of *worlds*. Murderers of all life. Hated and feared throughout the galaxy. They are a plague

118

that spreads from world to world, leaving nothing but desolation and slavery and misery in their wake.>

I felt cold. Small and weak and cold and afraid. I looked around, but even the inviting, lush Andalite landscape did nothing to warm me. Up in the "sky" and all around us, I felt the immense pressure of the ocean, waiting to rush in.

<There are only three races left in all the known galaxy that still fight the Yeerks,> Ax said proudly. <And only the Andalites can stop them.>

"How long until your people return to Earth?" I asked.

He hesitated. <One of your years. Maybe two.>

"Two years!" Jake looked stricken. I went to his side and slipped my arm through his. "Five kids against an enemy that has destroyed half the galaxy? Five of us?"

Ax gave that smile, the one he did with his eyes. <Six, my Prince,> he said.

"Six. Well then," Marco said with grim sarcasm, "with *six* it shouldn't be any problem."

"How did these Yeerks get this far?" Rachel demanded. "How did this happen? If you Andalites are so tough, why didn't you stop them a long time ago? How did a bunch of slugs who live in dirty ponds manage to become so powerful?"

Ax looked at her. <I am forbidden to tell certain things.>

Rachel's eyes narrowed dangerously. "You're telling us all of planet Earth may be scheduled for destruction and we are the only thing standing in the way, and you are going to keep secrets? I don't think so."

The Andalite looked angry, but no angrier than Rachel.

"Look, um, I feel ready to morph again," I said, interrupting the tension. Rachel was angry because she was afraid. What Ax had told us had shaken her. It had shaken all of us. I guess we felt enough pressure already. We didn't really need to think that every living thing on the planet was depending on us.

It was kind of a lot to handle.

"Cassie's right," Jake said. "It's time. Let's get going before it's too late."

I followed him along with the others as we crossed alien land, heading for an environment just as alien — the ocean.

I wished I could forget what Ax told us. I wished I could stop seeing the pictures in my head of an Earth without birds and trees. An Earth where the ocean was empty and dead.

<Don't you know whom you're fighting?> the Andalite had asked.

Yes.

Now I knew.

CHAPTER 20

"Hey, I have a stupid question," Marco said.

"What?" Jake asked.

Marco jerked his thumb toward the Andalite, Ax. "How do we get him out of here?"

Jake looked blank. "Um, Ax, I don't suppose you can swim? Swim really well, I mean. We're a long, long way from land."

<I would not swim in this body. I would morph a sea creature.>

"Like what?" Marco asked bluntly. "We have to travel far and fast."

<I have acquired a creature from this ocean. It was a large creature who swam close one day. I stunned him and acquired him. I thought he would be useful if I was to escape.>

"What kind of animal? What did he —" I stopped suddenly. I'd felt something. A shadow. I looked up. Through the air of the dome. Through the clear dome itself and up through the water.

It was on the surface. A cigar-shaped shadow riding the surface of the sea.

"That's a ship," I said. "Up there. I think it's stopped."

"Let's get out of here. Now," Jake snapped.

We ran for the hatch.

PING-NG-NG! PING-NG-NG!

The sound echoed through the dome.

"Sonar!" Marco hissed.

"How do you know?" Rachel asked.

"Didn't you ever see *The Hunt for Red October*? Great movie. Now let's leave. They've found us!"

PING-NG-NG! PING-NG-NG!

We crammed inside the small hatch enclosure, the four of us and Ax.

"Morph!" Jake yelled.

I had already started. I could feel the dolphin features emerging. My friends were beginning to mutate. Water rushed into the chamber, swirling up around our legs.

Ax was changing, too. It almost broke my concentration, watching him. In their normal forms Andalites are strange enough. When they morph it is totally bizarre. Instead of two legs shriveling and disappearing, it was four. And then there were the stalk eyes. And the tail, which lost its scythe blade but split into a new kind of tail, with a long, raked, vertical blade and a shorter lower blade.

The water swept up to my neck, but by that point I was more dolphin than human.

BA-BOOOOM!

The explosion shuddered through the dome. It rattled my teeth. I felt like my eardrums would explode.

<Yeerks,> Ax said. He said the word in our heads the way his brother had. With hatred and rage so deep it was impossible to comprehend it.

BA-BOOOOM!

A second explosion! Suddenly the exterior door opened and we swam out in a rush. Four dolphins and one . . .

Shark!

I'd been distracted by the explosions.

Ax had morphed a shark.

<Oh, good choice, Ax,> Marco said. <You morphed a *shark*?>

<Is it wrong?> the Andalite wondered.

<Your species and ours are mortal enemies,> I explained.

<Oh. I have a lot to learn about Earth.>

<Here's the first lesson — let's get OUT OF HERE!> Marco screamed.

I soared up through the water, angling toward the distant surface. But as I rose I looked behind me. There were two jagged holes in the dome. Water was gushing in like Niagara Falls. As I watched, a third dark cylinder was falling slowly from the surface. Even I had seen enough submarine movies to know it was a depth charge.

<What hosts have these Yeerks used?> Ax demanded urgently.

<Um . . . Hosts? You mean bodies? Controllers? They use Hork-Bajir and humans,> I answered.

<Hork-Bajir do not swim,> Ax said. <We may be safe. The Yeerks know little of deep waters. They have no oceans on their world, only shallow pools.>

<Good,> Jake said. <All they've had here are Hork-Bajir. And Taxxons, of course.>

<Taxxons?>

<Yes, is that a problem?>

We were near the surface now, just a dozen feet from the bright barrier of sea and sky.

Just then a larger, darker shadow swept over us. A shadow that was dark inside of dark. A shadow that touched your soul. It skimmed just above the surface of the water.

It was shaped like a long battle-ax. Twin semicircular blades at the back, a long, diamond-headed point at the front.

The Blade ship of Visser Three.

Something was falling from it as it passed over us. There were a dozen splashes. I rolled over to get a better look.

What I saw made my flesh crawl.

Taxxons. In the water. Coming toward us.

<Those nasty worms can *swim*?> Marco yelled.

But the answer was obvious. The Taxxons, ten-foot-long centipedes bristling with dozens of pairs of sharp needle legs, were racing after us. And they were very fast in the water.

Very fast.

From this angle we couldn't see the several red-jelly eyes. But we could see the circular mouth at the top of each vile body.

I had seen Taxxons straining to catch bits of Prince Elfangor as Visser Three devoured him.

I had seen Taxxons, on orders from Visser Three, devour one of their own.

<Tell me,> Ax said. <I have the feeling that this body I am in might be able to fight. Is this true?>

I grinned inwardly. <Yes, Ax. Sharks can fight.>

<Then, Prince Jake, shall we deal with these Taxxon scum?>

<Don't call me 'prince,'> Jake said. <And the answer is yes. Let's go kick some Taxxon butt.>

CHAPTER 21

There were a dozen Taxxons in the water. Five of us. Swimming in a straight line, the Taxxons were faster. But, as we soon discovered, we were more maneuverable.

<Pick a target,> Jake said tersely.

I focused on one of the big worms. But I had to force myself into the fight. This was not a shark, and the dolphin's instinctive dislike of sharks was not there to prod me.

I had to find the will to fight in my own, human mind. It's not such an easy thing. I had fought the Yeerks to preserve human freedom. Now I fought to help the entire world. Still, fighting doesn't come naturally to me.

And yet, I knew what I had to do. The Yeerks would show no mercy. If the Taxxons won, we would be killed. Or worse.

I powered toward one of the Taxxons as he powered toward me. We were like two trains running on the same track. Head to head.

At the last possible second, with the gaping red mouth of the Taxxon just a foot away, I zoomed sideways, arched my back, and rammed the Taxxon's side.

I expected it to be like the shark — hard, tough, unyielding. It was not. It was like hitting a soggy paper bag with a sledgehammer. The Taxxon burst like a dropped watermelon.

<Aaaaarrrggghhh!> I wanted to throw up. I beat the water with my tail and recoiled from the horrible scene I had created.

All around me the battle raged. Dolphin against Taxxon. And Ax's shark against Taxxon.

Scientists believe that sharks are one of the oldest species of animals still in existence. Nature built them as perfect predators. Perfect killing machines. Nature hasn't had to revise or update them much. They were built right the first time.

Dolphins are very different. Scientists say that millions of years ago, dolphins were land animals. Sea mammals not very different from humans and other mammals. They evolved their way back into the ocean. Part of that evolution included learning to cope with predators — with killer whales and sharks.

I don't know what sea the Taxxon race evolved in. I don't know what natural predators they faced there. But they were not ready for this ocean. They were not ready to go one-on-one with the masters of Earth's deep seas. They were no match for dolphin or shark.

<Okay, let's get out of here,> Jake ordered. <They've had enough.>

<Not so tough, are they?> Rachel asked, trying to sound tough herself. But she seemed shaky to me.

I shot to the surface and filled my lungs with warm evening air. The sun was dropping toward the horizon. Two ships were close by and steaming in our direction.

But far worse was the Blade ship, which hovered now just a hundred yards up in the air.

<We can't waste any more time,> Marco said. <The plan was to head back for one of those little channel islands, unmorph, rest, and then take the rest of the distance. But even the island is almost two hours away at top speed. We have to make a run for it, or we'll have to choose between being trapped in morph or drowning. And that's not a great choice.>

<You're right, Marco,> Jake said. <Top speed for the nearest island.>

<How do you tell the time?> Ax asked.

<Sometimes we can carry a watch. Sometimes, like now, we just have to guess and hope for the best.>

<Oh. With your permission, I will keep track of the time.>

<You have a watch?>

<No, but I have the ability to keep track of time,> Ax said.

<Good enough,> Marco said. <How much time left?>

<We have been in morph for approximately thirty percent of the safe time.>

<Thirty percent?> I tried to think. Math was never my best subject. And it's hard to be mathematical when you've just come from a battle and are scared half to death. <That would be about thirty-six minutes. Which means we have an hour and twenty-four minutes left.>

BAH-LUMPH!

I heard a huge concussion behind me. Like someone had dropped a big truck in the water.

<What was that?> Marco wondered.

<Something hit the water,> I said. <Something big.>

WHUMP, WHUMP, WHUMP.

<Okay, now what is *that*?> Rachel asked.

I rose to the surface to breathe and look around. The two surface ships were still closing in, but they were not very fast, and they were not gaining on us. The Blade ship had disappeared. I scanned the sky in all directions, but I couldn't see it.

<Does anyone see the Blade ship?> I asked.

<No. But that doesn't mean it isn't still nearby,> Jake said. <It may have recloaked.>

WHUMP, WHUMP, WHUMP.

<What is that?>

<Whatever it is, it's getting closer,> I said.

Suddenly I remembered that I was not limited to the usual human senses. I fired off a rapid series of echolocating clicks.

The picture that came back was startling.

<It's something in the water. Big. Huge. The size of a whale, but not moving like a whale.>

Jake, Marco, and Rachel all echolocated.

<It's after us, whatever it is,> Rachel said.

<It's big, it's fast, and it's after us,> Marco agreed.

WHUMP, WHUMP, WHUMP.

I rose to breathe again and looked back. At just that moment I saw, far behind me, a huge, dark red, almost purple hump above the water. It seemed to be covered with hundreds of small fish tails, all beating frantically.

I went under. <Ax, there's something back there. I don't think it's from Earth.> I described it to him, at least what I had seen of it.

<Mardrut,> Ax said.

<Mardrut? What does that mean?>

<A mardrut is a beast that lives in the oceans of one of our own Andalite moons. To think of that filthy Yeerk scum on our own moon! Acquiring our animals!>

<Ax, look, what is a mardrut?> I asked him.

<It is a very large creature that swims by shooting water out of three large chambers. It makes a sound —>

WHUMP, WHUMP, WHUMP.

<A sound like that?> Marco asked.

<Yes,> Ax said. <I guess so. I did not recognize it. I have only heard it once, and that was in school, and I wasn't paying attention.>

It almost made me laugh, the image of an Andalite classroom where Andalite students zoned out on the lesson just like we did. But it really wasn't a good time for laughing.

WHUMP, WHUMP, WHUMP.

<But this is no true mardrut,> Ax said.

<No,> Jake agreed.

<Then you know who and what is chasing us?> Ax seemed surprised. <You understand that this is Visser Three in morph?>

<We've met before,> Rachel said tersely.

<You have fought Visser Three? And you still live?> That definitely surprised the Andalite. <I honor you.>

<Yeah, swell, thanks,> Marco said dryly. <But I'd trade the honor for a good outboard engine so I could outrun that evil creep.>

WHUMP, WHUMP, WHUMP.

CHAPTER 22

The creature Visser Three had become did not tire.

We *did*.

I felt like I had been swimming forever. Half an hour into the chase, I was exhausted. We had been powering through the water at panic speed. Fighting every current. Fighting the terrible urge to rest as our tails weakened. Fighting the growing hunger.

WHUMP, WHUMP, WHUMP.

The mardrut never tired. It never weakened. It gained on us a foot at a time, bit by bit.

I could see it now. A huge purple-and-red mottled bag that undulated and oozed through the water. It was propelled by the three huge water sacs, firing one after another. Between those loud bursts, the hundreds of tiny tails that covered its entire surface thrashed and kept up momentum.

WHUMP, WHUMP, WHUMP.

Then he spoke. We had all heard that silent voice in our heads before. It was like hearing the most terrible curses. It was pure malice and hatred poured directly into our brains.

<I am coming for you, brave Andalite warriors,> Visser Three sneered. <I am coming for you.>

That voice churned my insides. I felt my own hatred flaring up to match his. The images Ax had painted — an Earth brown and empty and filled with nothing but the slaves of the Yeerks. . . .

I had lived my entire life without feeling hatred. It is a sickening feeling. It burns and burns, and sometimes you think it's a fire that will never go out.

<I am coming for you. You will be mine. Shall I make you Controllers? Or shall I simply eat you? The time for me to decide draws near. You weaken. Your time runs short.>

WHUMP, WHUMP, WHUMP.

We had all been exposed to Visser Three. Ax had not. He seemed to shudder, even in his shark body. The dead shark eyes showed no emotion, but his swimming became erratic.

<Ax,> I said to him. He did not answer. <Ax, we have heard his voice before. We've heard his threats. And we are still alive.>

<He will kill us,> Ax said. <He will kill us! He killed Elfangor!>

<Ax, hang in there. Don't answer him. Don't think about him. Just swim!>

But Ax's fear was catching. He was right. We didn't have enough time to make it to land without being trapped in our dolphin bodies. And we would never escape him, anyway. I glanced back.

He was only five body lengths away!

I demanded still more from my burning muscles, but there was nothing more to ask.

This is the end, Cassie, I told myself. *This is the end.*

I felt the terrible hatred surge in me again. But I didn't want to end my life that way. I would not die with hate in my heart. That would be one victory I could deny Visser Three.

I let my mind drift, even as my shattered body struggled to go on. I felt my mind floating back. To the barn, and all the animals there. To my father, my mother. To Jake.

I remembered good things. Riding the high thermals with Tobias and the others with wings

135

spread wide. Good days. Sitting at my grand-mother's feet as she told me the story of our family, of all the generations who had lived on and worked the farm.

And then a more recent memory surfaced. The whale. I remembered his huge, gentle silence filling my mind.

I could even hear his song.

Wait! I *could* hear his song. That wasn't memory. I was hearing his plaintive, haunting song, reverberating through the water.

He was not far away.

I opened my mind and let my human consciousness slip away. I let go. I invited the dolphin mind — the mind that loved to play and loved to fight and loved the feeling of soaring out of the water right up into the air like a bird — to surface in my head.

I fired echolocating bursts, a thousand quick clicks compressed into a few seconds. And more than that, I cried for help.

It was foolish. It was ridiculous. But I cried out in a silent plea, like a child with a nightmare calling for her mother.

The monster is after me! The destroyer! The evil one!

Help me.

<We have used eighty percent of our time,> Ax managed to say.

<Twenty-four minutes left,> Marco gasped.

<It doesn't matter. I'm done for,> Rachel admitted. <I can't keep going. And he's too close. It's time to turn and fight.>

WHUMP, WHUMP, WHUMP.

<We cannot possibly win,> Ax said.

<We know,> Jake said. <But if I have to lose, I'd rather lose fighting than let him catch us one by one.>

<That is a very Andalite thing to say,> Ax said. <We have a lot in common. I wish it had ended differently.>

<On the count of three,> Jake said.

<One.>

<Two.>

<Let's go.>

We stopped. We turned to face the mardrut.

<Jake?> I said. <I wanted to tell you . . .>

<Yes. Me, too, Cassie,> he said.

WHUMP, WHUMP, WHUMP.

The red-and-purple behemoth rushed at us.

I shook with terror. But I was too tired to swim away.

Help me! I cried one last time. But I knew there was no one to help.

And then I let it all go . . .

. . . and said good-bye.

CHAPTER 23

<I've made up my mind what to do with you,> Visser Three said. <After this long chase I am really quite hungry.>

He rushed at us.

We rushed at him.

Something dark came hurtling up from the ocean floor.

Something dark and long and bigger even than the mardrut.

FWOOOMP!

Visser Three shuddered and stopped dead in the water.

A second dark shape, as fast as the first.

FWOOOMP!

<The *great ones*,> I whispered.

<It's the whales!> Marco yelled.

There were five of them in the water.

The two big males who had struck first had heads like sledgehammers. Sperm whales. Sixty feet long. Sixty-five tons. The weight of fifty cars.

They had dived deep and come tearing up at awesome velocity to slam into the creature from another world's ocean.

The mardrut was big. The mardrut was strong. But nothing living can survive for long, being slammed by creatures weighing a hundred and thirty thousand pounds.

Then, the whale — my whale, because that's how I thought of him — began to lash the mardrut with his tail. Hammer blows. Hits that could have knocked walls down. Again and again, as two smaller females joined in and the two sperm whales circled back for another attack.

<Rrraaaggghhhh!> Visser Three's cry of pain and fury echoed in my brain.

<He's retreating!> Jake crowed.

<He's running!> Rachel said. <Hah-hah!>

<I don't think Visser Three likes whales very much,> Marco yelled. <I don't think he likes them at all!>

The whales chased him for a while, but they let him go in the end.

Whales are not very good at killing. They don't really have much of a talent for hating and destroying.

My whale, the big humpback, returned in a few minutes and rested in the water beside me.

I wanted to thank him, but, as I said, whales don't think in human words or human thoughts. Still, I tried, anyway.

Thanks, big guy.

People who argue about how smart whales are, or whether they are as smart as humans, kind of miss the point. Whales will never read books or build rockets or do algebra. In all those areas, humans are smarter. Humans are the great brains of planet Earth.

But it isn't necessary to believe whales are as smart as humans to believe that they are great. They don't have to know words to sing songs. They don't have to be anything but what they are to be magnificent. And even though I don't really know what a soul is, I know this — if humans have them, then so do whales.

I wanted to thank him for responding to my call for help. But I had a strange feeling, as he opened his great heart to the dolphin mind that was in my own, that he hadn't just come in response to me.

I had the feeling — and that's all it was, a

feeling — that in some way the sea itself had called him to respond to the presence of an abomination.

Of course I never told that to Jake or any of the others. They would have laughed. At least, Marco would have.

<Morph time is almost up,> Ax said.

<I think if we morph, the whale will carry us until we are ready to morph again,> I said.

So we morphed back to our human bodies, and Ax morphed to his Andalite body, and we crawled up on the whale's huge back.

I fell asleep. I know that sounds pretty incredible, but I did. I was exhausted. Physically. Emotionally. In every way you can be tired, I was tired.

When I woke up, it was sunset. We were near shore. I could see the beach, and just a little farther down the shore, the mouth of the river.

We were wet, of course, covered with splashing water and the spray from the whale's blowhole. It was a little cold, especially now that the sun was going down.

But then again, I wasn't Visser Three's lunch, so I wasn't going to complain.

Jake was sitting cross-legged on the whale's back, smiling at me.

"Some day, huh?" he said.

I smiled. "Yeah."

"We did it. We saved the Andalite. And we got out alive."

"Barely," I said.

"You know something? You were right. You trusted your feelings and we followed you and we're all safe."

I nodded. "Yes, I guess so. Only . . . as Marco would say, let's not do this again any time soon, okay?"

Jake smiled his slow smile. "It's fun being a dolphin, though, isn't it? I know you were worried about it. You know, thinking maybe it wasn't right and all."

I shook my head slowly. "I'm still not sure it's right. But I guess we don't have much of a choice. The Yeerks started this fight, not us. And after what Ax said . . . I guess it's not just about one species, human beings. It's about all the animals. It's about all of Earth."

Jake nodded. "I think if you could ask the dolphins, they would say it's all right to use them. Since what you're trying to do is save them."

"Nah, they would just think it was all a big game. They would never understand."

We both laughed. Even if they could talk, the dolphins would never really understand what we were so upset about. We knew that better than anyone.

"I guess that's true," Jake said. "But we do understand." He met my gaze. "We do understand what's at stake. And we'll do whatever we have to do to win."

I knew what he was trying to tell me. We'd used the dolphins to save them. We'd used other animals to save them, too. And that made it okay.

CHAPTER 24

We morphed once more into our dolphin bodies and swam down the river to the place where we had entered the water. We beached ourselves in shallow water and returned to our human bodies.

"It feels good to be human again," Jake said.

Marco said, "Oh, Jake, you were never exactly human to begin with."

I guess it was funny, but we were all too tired to laugh.

We dug our clothes and shoes out of their hiding place. I pulled jeans and a sweatshirt on over my wet morphing suit. I shoved muddy feet into my boots.

<Strange,> Ax said, watching us very closely.

<What is the meaning of the things you place on your bodies?>

"It's clothing," Rachel explained.

<Why do you wear it? Does it protect you from the environment?>

"Yes. That, plus the fact that people get very upset if you walk around naked," Marco answered.

There was a fluttering overhead. One of the shadowed branches dipped with a sudden weight.

"Is that you, Tobias?" I asked.

<Yes. You . . . you found an Andalite!>

"Yes. Tobias, meet Ax. That's his nickname, anyway. Ax, meet Tobias. Tobias is one of us."

<Sort of, anyway,> Tobias said dryly. <I liked this morph so much I moved in permanently.>

The Andalite was shocked. <You were trapped?>

<Yes.>

Ax turned his eyes on me, then looked from each one of us to the next. He seemed very solemn. <You have paid a price for the gift of my brother, Elfangor.>

<Prince Elfangor was your brother?> Tobias demanded. His hawk's eyes glittered. <I was with him at the end.>

"This is all fine," Jake interrupted, "but we have to get out of here. And we have to decide what to do with Ax. He can't exactly just go walking through town with us."

"I think he should come to my farm," I said. "It's not so different from the dome ship. Fields, meadows, woods, all the way into the national forest land. He'd have to be careful, but it's the only place we have to hide him."

"That still doesn't deal with how we're going to get him there," Marco pointed out. "It's a long walk. People are gonna notice a big blue deer with extra eyes and a scorpion tail."

<I must morph,> Ax said.

"Yeah, but into what?" Rachel wondered.

Then, to my surprise, Ax walked over to me. He placed one delicate, many-fingered hand on my face.

<With your permission,> he said.

I felt myself getting spacey. Not sleepy, exactly, but sort of like I was in a trance.

I realized what he was doing. He was "acquiring" me. He was absorbing my DNA.

"Um . . . excuse me, but you're going to morph Cassie?" Marco asked. "Can you do that?"

Ax went to Marco and touched his face. One by one, Ax acquired each of us.

And then he began to morph.

I've seen a lot of strange morphings. But nothing was ever like this. Ax wasn't becoming an animal. He was becoming a human being.

But a human being we all knew, in some ways. A melding of the four human Animorphs.

His front legs began to shrivel away. His back legs thickened and strengthened. Suddenly a mouth appeared in his Andalite face.

The scorpion tail shrank and disappeared.

He reared up and stood erect.

"Um, you know, I think we better give Ax some privacy," I suggested.

"Is he going to be a boy or a girl?" Marco wondered.

"Either way, let's turn our heads," I said.

We did. Probably just in time.

"Hey, Ax? In the pile of clothes there is an extra pair of boxers and a T-shirt," Jake said. "Put them on, okay?"

A few minutes later we turned around. We all stared.

Ax had the T-shirt pulled up like a baggy pair of shorts. The boxers were on his head.

"O-o-o-o-kay," Jake said. "A few small adjustments needed. Ax, are you male or female?"

"I chose to be-be-be-be-be male." He stopped suddenly, eyes wide. He was surprised by his mouth. It was not something Andalites understood.

"I chose male because I am male. Word. Male. Is that a good choice? Ch-oy-ce? Chuh chuh choy-yuss?" He twisted his lips around and stuck out his tongue. "Strange," he said.

"Male is fine," Jake said. "Rachel? Cassie?

147

Turn around. Marco and I will help Ax adjust his clothing."

When I looked again, Ax was dressed normally.

But he did not *look* normal. He was of medium height, a perfect balance between Rachel and Marco. He was of medium build, somewhere between Jake and Marco. His hair was brown, with just a little of Rachel's gold and a little of my curl. His skin was the color of light brown sugar, a blending of my brown and Marco's olive, and Jake and Rachel's pale white.

He was human and yet, somehow, strange.

He jerked his head this way and that. "How do you look? Lookuh. LooKUH. KUH. How do you look around? Ound. Ow, ow, ownd behind?"

I grinned. It was exactly like every time I first morphed a new animal. He was getting used to his new body. Or at least trying to. As I watched him play with his lips and try out new sounds, he suddenly tumbled forward.

Jake grabbed him and held him.

"You only have two legs now, Ax," he said.

"Yes. Two. Oo. Very shaky."

"Yeah, we're a shaky species," Marco said.

"Well, let's get out of here," Jake said.

"Ax?" I said. "Don't talk to any strangers on the way home, okay?"

CHAPTER 25

It was a couple of days later. After we had recovered. After I had made sure that Ax was safe in the far fields of our farm, away from curious eyes.

I waited till dark, and changed again into the seagull morph.

I flew out of my barn and through the night to The Gardens.

It was closed and empty, aside from a few scattered security guards. They would have stopped me if I had tried to enter normally. But no one was looking out for seagulls.

I landed near the dolphin tank and became human again. There were no lights on and just a sliver of moon, but I could hear the dolphins swimming. One came over to me, curious about why a human would be hanging around at night.

"Hi," I said. "Sorry, I don't have any food for you."

Then I climbed up on the side of the tank. I let myself go, slipping into the cool water.

Three of the dolphins came over to take a look. This was definitely something unusual. Some strange human was getting in the pool with them. This was a new game.

I began to morph.

This definitely got their attention. All six dolphins swam around, looking up at me, sideways at me, back at me as they passed.

And slowly I became one of them.

It was a dumb thing to do, really. I knew it was dumb. But it felt like something I had to do.

I wanted to show them what I had done. I wanted their permission to become one of them. I wanted to find some way to tell them . . . everything.

But you know, once I was in that dolphin body again, it was hard to remember all my solemn worries. It was hard to remember why I had come.

Hard to remember fear and worry and guilt.

One of them came over, gave me a nudge, then shot toward the surface. She exploded into the air and fell back, as silent and smooth as an arrow.

They were asking me to play.
They were asking me to dance with them.
And so I did.

#5 The Predator

"Stop!" a cop yelled. "I'm ordering you to halt!"

But Ax wasn't interested in halting. He was panicked.

A woman stepped out of the Body Shop holding a bag full of colorful jars. Ax plowed into her. The bag went flying.

The stalks began to grow out of the top of his head. The extra eyes appeared on the ends and turned backward to watch the people chasing him.

Jake and I were two of those people. We were ahead of the cops, but not by much. Fortunately, I guess the cops assumed we were just idiots running along for fun.

I could hear one of the cops yelling into his walkie-talkie. "Cut him off at the east entrance!"

Legs began to grow from the chest of Ax's human morph. His own front legs, small at first, but growing rapidly.

He was slowing down as his human legs began to change. The knees were reversing direction. His spine elongated into the beginnings of a tail.

Then's when the screaming started.

"Ahhh ahhhhh!"

"What is it? What IS it?"

People were screaming and running and dropping their bags as they caught sight of the nightmare creature Ax had become. Half-human, half-Andalite. A fluid, shifting mess of half-formed features.

I couldn't blame them. I felt like screaming myself.

. . . Suddenly, Ax fell forward, tangled up in his own mutating legs. He skidded down the polished marble floor. . . .

"You kids get out of the way!" one of them yelled at us. "This guy could be dangerous."

Ax sprang up. He was much more sure of himself, now that he was on his four Andalite hooves. . . .

It was then that I heard the nearest mall cop, in an awed frightened whisper, say, "Andalite!"

I quickly turned and looked at him. Only a Controller would recognize an Andalite. The Controller cop drew his gun from his holster.

"RUN!" I yelled at Ax. . . .

ANIC06